'You could welcoming, Alis

Luke's eyes moved and she felt herself tremble.

'What do you want from me, Luke?' she asked huskily.

'I've already told you. I want to see my son.'

'And I've told you, my life and my child are none of your business.'

Luke shook his head. 'I really think you should reconsider…' There was a dangerous warning hidden behind the softness of his tone and it wasn't lost on her. 'I've come here today in an act of friendship, to ask you politely about Nathan—'

'And I've answered you politely.'

'You've answered nothing. And quite frankly, Alison, my patience is wearing thin. I wouldn't advise you to mess me around any further.'

'I'm not afraid of you, Luke,' Alison replied, her eyes blazing into his now.

'Well, maybe you should be,' Luke said quietly. 'Because when I want something I usually get it…'

Kathryn Ross was born in Zambia, where her parents happened to live at that time. Educated in Ireland and England, she now lives in a village near Blackpool, Lancashire. Kathryn is a professional beauty therapist, but writing is her first love. As a child she wrote adventure stories, and at thirteen was editor of her school magazine. Happily, ten writing years later, DESIGNED WITH LOVE was accepted by Mills & Boon®. A romantic Sagittarian, she loves travelling to exotic locations.

Recent titles by the same author:

THE ELEVENTH-HOUR GROOM
THE NIGHT OF THE WEDDING
HER DETERMINED HUSBAND
THE MILLIONAIRE'S AGENDA

THE SECRET CHILD

BY
KATHRYN ROSS

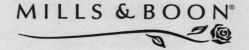

MILLS & BOON®

MILLS & BOON and MILLS & BOON with the Rose Device are registered trademarks of the publisher.

First published in Great Britain 2002
Harlequin Mills & Boon Limited,
Eton House, 18-24 Paradise Road, Richmond, Surrey TW9 1SR

© Kathryn Ross 2002

ISBN 0 263 82974 X

Set in Times Roman 10½ on 12 pt.
01-1002-48984

Printed and bound in Spain
by Litografia Rosés, S.A., Barcelona

CHAPTER ONE

HE WAS her ex-lover and he was now a married man. Both were good reasons to try to forget Luke Davenport, except for the fact that Alison had far greater cause to remember him.

She opened the lattice window of her cottage and took a deep breath of the early-morning air, but it was warm and sticky and did little to relieve the stifling feeling of unease inside her. There was a storm brewing, she thought, her eyes moving to the milky mist that hung over the ocean and the Cornish cliffs. It was as if the whole world was holding its breath because Luke Davenport had come home.

Nathan dropped his spoon on the tiled floor and Alison turned her attention back to the kitchen.

'Oh, dear!' She smiled at him and he smiled back, a spark of mischief in his big blue eyes. Was her son exceptionally gorgeous, Alison wondered dreamily, or did every mother think that about her child? She bent to pick up the spoon and rinsed it under the tap.

'Shall Mummy help you with breakfast?' she asked him, sitting down at the table beside him and spooning up a little of the baby food to hold it out temptingly. Nathan shook his head then reached out and took the spoon from her.

'OK, Mr Independent.'

Alison sipped her tea and tried to dismiss the fact that Luke was home, but as she watched Nathan in his high chair she knew that was easier said than done. Nathan's blue eyes and dark hair reminded her so much of his father that sometimes it made her heart squeeze with pain.

In a few weeks he would be two. The way time was flying he would soon be at an age to ask questions about his father, and then what would she tell him? That Luke hadn't wanted him? That was a lie. Luke hadn't wanted her...but he knew nothing of his child. For Nathan's sake she wished things could have been different.

But things couldn't be different, she told herself firmly. Luke was married and he was only home for a short while to attend his father's funeral and sort out the family estate then he would be returning to New York again.

Even for Nathan's sake she couldn't get in contact with him now. Who knew what demons she would be unleashing? It was two and a half years since she had last seen Luke and that meeting had not been pleasant. She had enough problems at the moment without conjuring up Luke Davenport as well, she thought furiously.

Dragging her mind away from thoughts of Luke, Alison glanced at the clock. It was seven-thirty; soon her child-minder, Jane, would arrive and she could leave for work. Ahead of her lay a gruelling day, including a change-over of guests at the hotel and an important meeting with the bank manager. She would be lucky if she got home in time to tuck Nathan up in his cot. In all probability he would be fast asleep when she got back.

'I don't want to go to work today, Nathan,' she groaned. 'I wish I could stay here with you.'

Nathan chuckled as if this was a great joke.

But it wasn't really funny. Work seemed beset with problems these days and she seemed to be spending longer and longer hours there. That was the trouble with a family business, she supposed, it was very difficult to just clock off when you had done the required amount of hours. The hotel was almost like having another child, she felt responsible for it…had a duty of care towards it, because it wasn't just her own monetary position that was on the line but her brothers' as well. They all had a stake in the Cliff House Hotel, and if it went under they were all in trouble.

The shrill ring of the phone cut into her thoughts and she reached to pick it up.

'Hi, sis, how are you this fine morning?'

It took a moment for Alison to recognise the cheerful tones of her elder brother. These days she was so used to Garth's voice being weighed down with the problems of the business that this was a complete surprise. 'Hi; you sound happy.'

'That's because I am happy, sis… I really am.' He almost sang the words. 'I think I've solved all our business problems.'

Alison frowned. She had been going over the accounts again last night and knew full well that things were even more serious than they had first feared. 'Short of a miracle, Garth, I don't see how—'

'It is a miracle… I've found an investor, someone who is going to make all the difference in the world to us. I can't give you facts at the moment because I have a few details to sort out first…but as soon as I have a solid deal to put on the table I'll call a family meeting. Will you phone the bank and see if you can stall this meeting with the manager until the end of the week?'

'Well, I'll try… Who is this mysterious investor? You know we have to be careful about bringing in another partner—'

'I'll talk to you about it later. Thanks, Alison.' The
phone went dead.

Now, what was that all about? Alison wondered as
she put the receiver down. The hotel was in such dire
straits that she couldn't see any investor in their right
minds wanting to bail them out. She hoped Garth wasn't
building himself up for a big disappointment.

But there wasn't time to think about it because Jane
arrived and with her usual efficient manner seemed to
take over the cottage. Alison picked up her briefcase and
kissed Nathan goodbye.

It didn't take long to drive down the narrow country
lanes to the hotel. As she pulled into her parking space
the first thing she noticed was the bright red Mercedes
sports car parked next to her.

It was such an attractive, head-turning car that she
glanced at it again as she walked across the gravel towards the entrance of the hotel. That was when she noticed the personalised number plate. LUKE 1.

A *frisson* of apprehension shot through her. It couldn't
be Luke Davenport's car…could it? What reason would
he have to come up to the hotel? It was hardly the place
he'd choose to drop in for morning coffee with his wife.

She continued on up the steps towards the revolving
glass doors. Even Luke didn't have that weird a sense
of humour.

Or maybe he'd found out about Nathan and curiosity
had brought him here? The very notion made her feel
slightly queasy but she continued walking into the lux-
urious foyer of the Cliff House.

Luke couldn't know about Nathan, she reassured herself. The only people who knew the truth were her brothers and her close friend Todd and none of them would
break her trust. And anyhow even if Luke did find out

about Nathan he wouldn't care, just as he hadn't cared about her.

He'd been back home to visit his father a year ago and she had gone through all these same anxieties then, but Luke hadn't bothered to contact her. He'd returned to the States and married Bianca.

'Morning, Alison.' The head receptionist looked up with a smile.

'Morning, Clare; how is everything today?' It was her standard greeting and she sounded remarkably cool but that wasn't how she was feeling; in truth, every nerve-ending seemed to be standing on edge.

'Everything's fine.' The woman smiled back. 'But you've got a visitor.'

'Have I?' Her heart was starting to pound heavily against her chest. 'Who?'

'I don't know. He didn't give his name.'

For a brief moment of giddy relief Alison thought she had got it wrong, that it wasn't him at all. Everyone in the village knew Luke Davenport.

Clare lowered her voice. 'But whoever he is, he's drop-dead gorgeous,' she whispered conspiratorially. 'He's waiting for you in the library.'

Drop-dead gorgeous…yes, that was an apt description of Luke Davenport, she thought bleakly, remembering that Clare was new to the village and wouldn't know him.

'OK…' Alison's brain was racing. 'Give me five minutes, then come through and tell me I have an important phone call.'

If Clare was puzzled by the request she didn't show it. 'Sure,' she said easily.

Just keep calm and you'll get through this, Alison told herself warily as she walked away from the reception

area. You're a twenty-five-year-old woman and Luke
Davenport doesn't have any power over you any more.

But the calm, sensible words were forgotten as she
walked into the library and saw Luke standing with his
back to her looking out of the windows towards the sea.

She stopped just inside the doorway and stared at the
tall, powerful figure. The very way he was standing, his
feet slightly apart, the way he was dressed in black jeans
and a dark T-shirt...it was all so familiar that she felt a
lump rising from nowhere in her throat. For a horrifying
moment she was scared to speak in case her voice gave
away the fact that her senses were in total chaos.

She wished there was someone else in the room, but
the vast library with its deep golden settees and book-
shelf-lined walls was depressingly empty.

She cleared her throat and he turned.

'Hello, Ali.'

She looked into his eyes, hardly able to believe that
the man who had haunted her waking thoughts as well
as her sleeping ones for two and a half years was actually here.

He was every bit as handsome as when she had last
seen him. His thick dark hair held only a few strands of
silver at the temples. His features were classically perfect, from piercing blue eyes and a strong, square jaw to
lips that had a sensual curve. She remembered how those
lips had once captured hers in a sweet torment of desire
before wrenching her mind firmly away from that direction.

They were different people now, she reminded herself
fiercely, and he was a married man.

'Luke...this is a surprise.' Her voice was surprisingly
steady.

'Is it?' He smiled, that crooked smile that had always

done strange things to her insides. 'I thought that you
would have been expecting me.'

She shrugged helplessly. 'I heard about your father's
death. I was sorry. But why would I expect you to call
here?'

He didn't answer her immediately; instead his eyes
flicked over her, studying her carefully, taking in the
wide green eyes and the striking strawberry-blonde hair
that was tied back in a French plait. She felt the intensity
of his gaze almost as if he were touching her as he
worked his way leisurely down over the slender lines of
her figure in the white linen suit, before his eyes returned
to her face, where they remained with a steely kind of
force that was really unnerving. 'How about for old
times' sake?'

Alison suddenly wished that her hair was loose and
she had something to hide behind, she had never felt
more exposed…more helplessly vulnerable.

'Quite frankly, the last place I'd expect to see you is
here in the Cliff House, on enemy territory.'

He smiled. 'It was our fathers who were enemies,
Alison, not us…as I recall we crossed those barriers a
long time ago.' He watched the flare of colour in her
skin with a barely concealed wry amusement that made
her temperature soar even higher.

'So how long are you home for?' She hadn't meant
to ask that question but curiosity forced it to her lips.

'Long enough.'

Long enough for what? she wondered. Long enough
to sort his father's estate out and put it on the market?
Long enough to cause havoc in her life?

'I'm rather busy, Luke,' she said, glancing at her
wrist-watch. 'So what can I do for you? I'm sure you're

not here just to relive the good old days.' Her voice dripped with sarcasm.

He shook his head. 'Dear me…after two and a half long years, I thought you might have managed to spare me at least…' he looked at his own watch '…five minutes of your precious time before getting someone to come in here and rescue you with some excuse.'

If the reception area weren't so far from where Luke was standing she'd have sworn he had overheard her conversation with Clare. 'What do you want, Luke?' she asked again, trying not to be disconcerted by how easily he was able to second guess her moves.

'Well, I would have thought that was obvious… I want to see you, of course,' he said quietly.

Luke had an incredibly sexy voice. It had always sent shivers of desire racing through her and she was appalled to find that nothing had changed, he could still turn her on with just a word…a smile…

'I hear you have become a mother since I last saw you.'

The quietly spoken words reverberated through her consciousness as if they had been amplified a million times over. And his eyes seemed to burn now.

'Yes…and I hear you've got married.' She countered the question as deftly as she could. 'Congratulations.'

Clare chose that moment to break in on them and Alison had never been so glad to see someone in all her life.

'Sorry to disturb you, Alison, but you're wanted urgently on the phone.' The woman looked from one to the other and then smiled warmly at Luke.

Luke smiled back at her.

'OK, Clare, thank you.'

Clare didn't appear to have heard her, because she stood where she was, still smiling dreamily at Luke.

'I said it was OK, Clare, tell whoever is on the phone that I'll be along in a few minutes.' Alison tried again, an edge of impatience in her tone. It had always been the same, women just seemed to fall at Luke's feet, and it really irritated Alison. He was big-headed enough without more adoration.

'Oh…right.' Clare seemed to drag her gaze away from Luke with the utmost reluctance and left the room.

'Well, it's been nice seeing you again, Luke, but I really must get on with my work now.'

'You have a son, I believe,' Luke continued as if the break in the conversation had never taken place.

'I'm flattered that you are so interested.' Her voice was light but it was a tremendous effort to keep it that way. 'Yes, I'm very lucky; I have a lovely baby boy and I'm very happy.' She glanced again at her watch, but it was purely an excuse to be able to wrench her eyes away from the intensity of his. 'I'd better go and take my call. Goodbye, Luke.' She turned away from him, her heart thudding violently against her chest as she walked towards the door.

She could feel him watching her.

'So…who is the father of this child?' He asked the question quietly before she reached the door.

Her steps faltered and stopped. This was it, the moment she had dreaded, the moment she had tried to tell herself would never come.

It was a tremendous effort of will to turn again and look at him, but she forced herself to do it because she knew that everything hinged on her giving the acting performance of her life.

She raised one eyebrow in derision. 'That's really none of your business, Luke.'

'Isn't it?'

The cool composure of his tone sent an even greater tremor of disquiet racing through her. Back over the years there had been more than a few occasions when she had wanted to contact him, tell him about Nathan, and behind that impulse had always been the daydream of Luke flying to her side, saying, 'Darling, how wonderful... I'm sorry I hurt you; I'm sorry about the past.'

But the day he got married that fantasy had died. And, looking at the cold disdain in his expression now, she realised just how ludicrously absurd it had been. Luke couldn't care less about her. 'No, it's not. My private life is my own business.' Her voice lifted, her tone stronger, clearer.

'Correct me if I'm wrong but I'm informed he will be two years old very soon?'

'That's right.' She met his eyes and then laughed, a tinkling, silvery sound in the tense silence. 'You're not thinking...?'

'I don't know what to think, Alison.' He moved suddenly, walking towards her with a gleam of purpose in his eye that made her long to turn tail and run. 'I only learnt of the child's exact age last night, and my source of information...a highly reliable source, I might add, informed me that there was an air of mystery surrounding the boy's parentage.'

'There is no mystery; I just don't want my private life bandied around the village, that's all. I told you, my personal life is nobody's concern except my own.'

'And the boy's father.'

'Well, that goes without saying—'

'Does it?'

'I have no secrets from Nathan's father.'

'So this mystery man knows about me, then, does he?' He asked the question with cold disdain. 'Knows that there is a question mark over the parentage of this child?'

'There is no question over the parentage of my son.' Alison's voice rose angrily. 'And if you are trying to suggest that he might be yours, then just forget it because he most certainly is not. For your information, Nathan was born prematurely—'

'Really?' Luke didn't sound fazed, and, more worryingly, he didn't sound the slightest bit interested in her protestations. 'So when can I come and see him?'

'See him?' She was so shocked by the request that it took a moment to gather her senses and in that time her mask dropped and her vulnerability showed all too clearly. 'Why on earth would you want to see him?'

'Why do you think?' Luke asked calmly.

She shrugged. 'Quite frankly I haven't the foggiest. I wouldn't have thought you were the slightest bit interested in babies. Doesn't really go with your tough businessman image, Luke.'

'Doesn't it?' He sounded unconcerned.

'No. What's the matter, is being back at home so boring that you feel compelled to visit the local baby population?'

'Just this baby,' Luke said with a grim determination. 'And on the contrary, being back at home is turning out to be remarkably enthralling. So, shall I call at your house tonight...say, eight o'clock?'

'Get lost, Luke.' She made to turn away from him but he reached out and caught hold of her arm, pulling her back towards him and holding her against his body. The close contact sent a jolt of shock reverberating through her.

The subtle yet familiar scent of his cologne assailed her senses. She looked up at him and couldn't help remembering that the last time she had been this close to Luke Davenport he had kissed her, stealing her senses from her and turning her on so much that she had been dizzy with need.

The strange thing was that he always seemed to have that effect on her; it was as if he put some kind of spell over her as soon as he came too close, exerted some fascination that made her long to be closer. She felt like a lemming drawn towards the edge of the cliff. Even now, the dangerous, wild side of her liked the familiar feel of his body just a whisper from hers.

'You could be a little more welcoming, Alison,' he drawled. His eyes moved over the softness of her lips and she felt herself tremble.

'What do you want from me, Luke?' she asked huskily, wrenching her eyes away from his in the vain hope of breaking the sudden weakness invading her body.

'I've already told you. I want to see…Nathan.'

'And I've told you, my life and my child are none of your business.'

Luke shook his head. 'I really think you should reconsider…' There was a dangerous warning hidden behind the softness of his tone and it wasn't lost on her. 'I've come here today in an act of friendship, to ask you politely about Nathan—'

'And I've answered you politely.'

'You've answered nothing.' He ground the words out tersely. 'And quite frankly, Alison, my patience is wearing thin. I wouldn't advise you to mess me around any further.'

'Is that some kind of threat?'

'It's more of a promise. I intend to see the boy and if you continue to obstruct me you will find that I can make life very difficult for you.'

'I'm not frightened of you Luke,' she said, jerking her head high, her eyes blazing into his now.

'Well, maybe you should be,' he said quietly. 'Because when I want something I usually get it.'

'Just go to hell.' She pulled her arm away from his and he released her easily.

'That's not very polite.'

'That's because I don't feel particularly polite.'

'Well, perhaps you should start working on your attitude problem. We can do things the easy way...or the hard way; it's up to you. I'll give you today to think about it.'

'I don't need to think about it.'

'I'm sure you do.' In total contrast to her Luke sounded very much in control. 'Maybe you should ask your brother Garth for some advice.'

Alison frowned. 'What has Garth got to do with this?'

'A trouble shared is a trouble halved...isn't that what they say? Or is it a debt shared is a debt halved?'

'Luke, what are you talking about?'

'I think you should ask Garth.' Luke turned away to walk towards the door. 'I'll expect to hear from you tonight with an invitation to your house. If I don't then reasonable negotiations are over.'

The door swung closed behind him, leaving Alison staring after him shaking inside, her worst fears realised. Obviously he strongly believed that Nathan was his; he hadn't even been sidetracked for a moment by her attempt to lie and say the birth was premature. Who had he been talking to? she wondered. He had mentioned

Garth…but Garth was too loyal to let her secret slip…
wasn't he?

She supposed she had been fooling herself that she
could keep the identity of Nathan's father a secret, and
that only a few select people needed to know the truth.
But it was inevitable that Luke would come back one
day and that he would put two and two together.

But it would just be a passing interest for him, she
told herself firmly. So if she kept her nerve and her cool
and didn't allow Luke to intimidate her…he would soon
grow tired of the subject; after all, Luke was married.

As soon as he had sorted whatever he had come to
sort, he would be going back to his wife in New York.

As Alison made her way through the foyer to her office a low growl of thunder outside heralded the ap-
proaching storm. She closed the door behind her and put
her briefcase down on her desk, noticing as she did that
she had been so tense her nails had dug into the palms
of her hands leaving deep gouges.

'This is as bad as it's going to get,' she told herself
calmly. 'Luke Davenport can't hurt me any more.' Another rumble of thunder loudly penetrated the room and
she transferred her attention to the window, watching the
white flashes of light out at sea. The storm was still a
long way off, and the air was even hotter and stickier
than before.

In her mind she heard Luke's voice again. 'I'll expect
to hear from you tonight with an invitation to your
house. If I don't then reasonable negotiations are over.'

The words sent a shiver running through her.

Why had he suggested she speak to Garth?

Suddenly she was remembering Garth's optimism on
the phone this morning, his bright assurance that their

troubles might be over because he had found an investor for the hotel.

Even as her mind grappled with the possibility that he had been talking about Luke she was rejecting the idea…it wouldn't be Luke…it couldn't be. No member of her family would ever do business with a Davenport. Hadn't she almost been thrown out of the family once for daring to consort with Luke? And Garth had been one of his chief opponents, had hated him almost as much as her father had.

The phone rang on her desk and she snatched it up.

'Hi, sis, did Clare pass on my message?'

'No. Listen, Garth, I'm glad you've phoned back. I've just had—'

'I don't have time to chat, Ali,' he interrupted hastily. 'I just wanted to say that Luke Davenport might call by the hotel today. If he does, will you show him around the place?'

'Show him around?' Alison's mouth felt dry inside. 'Why would I do that?'

'I know it's a bit of a strange request coming from me, but just trust me on this and show him around.'

'He's been here already and I told him to get lost.'

'You did what?' The relaxed and affable tone left Garth's voice. 'Why the hell did you do that?'

'Why the hell do you think? Luke isn't interested in the hotel. He was here to ask about Nathan.'

'On the contrary, Luke Davenport is very interested in the hotel; he told me he might be willing to invest in the place. You do realise that your actions this morning could ruin everything? He is our one chance of saving the place… Alison, are you there? Alison?'

Alison put the phone down; she couldn't speak…she couldn't even think straight any more. All she knew was that this was worse than any nightmare scenario she might have imagined.

CHAPTER TWO

THE office had a strange, darkish green cast to it thrown from the sky outside, but it could easily have been a reflection of her mood, Alison thought grimly as she reached to switch on her desk lamp.

The first thing she'd done after putting the phone down on Garth was phone Jane to tell her that under no circumstances was she to go out with Nathan today and nor was she to open the door to callers.

Jane probably thought she had suddenly turned into a completely neurotic mother, but whatever she thought she wisely kept it to herself.

Realistically speaking, Alison didn't for one moment think that Luke would go around to her house uninvited. He had issued his ultimatum and if she knew anything about the man she figured he would be sticking by it. But even so she felt better once she'd phoned Jane and played it safe.

Then she sat down in her office chair and tried to think sensibly about the situation. But all she could see were Luke's eyes as they blazed into hers. And all she could think was how far removed it all was from the way he used to look at her with teasing warmth and deep desire. Of course, she had just been a game as far as he was concerned; there had never been anything meaningful in their relationship...that had all been in her imagination.

The Davenports owned the prestigious estate that neighboured her parents' farm. Although Luke had grown up next door, so to speak, she hadn't seen much of him as they moved in separate social circles. And he was eight years older than her and from an early age he was away at a private boarding-school in London. But she had first become aware of him when she was sixteen. It had been a very ordinary incident; she'd dropped a bag of groceries on the way out of the village shop and he had stopped to help her pick things up.

She remembered smiling at him, thinking that she had never met anyone with such gorgeous blue eyes before, and suddenly the ordinary day had turned into something very special.

'Thank you,' she had said.

'That's OK.' He grinned at her and then said more seriously, 'How's your mother, Alison? I hear she's been very sick.'

It didn't surprise Alison that he knew. The village of Penray was tiny and everyone knew each other's business.

'She's in hospital at the moment.'

'I'm sorry to hear that.' He patted her shoulder. It was just a brotherly gesture…he was so much older and more sophisticated that he probably didn't even think twice about it. But Alison did.

'I'm here for a few weeks before I go back to work in London. Tell your dad if I can be of any assistance I'll come over.'

Her father, who had been watching from his car, berated her severely once she got into the passenger seat beside him.

'Don't ever let me catch you talking to a Davenport again.' He ground the words out with bitter rancour.

'He was just being nice and he asked about Mum. Said to tell you if you need anything—'

'We don't need anything from the Davenports. Just

keep away from them, Alison. They are nothing but trouble. My brother would be alive today if it weren't for them.'

Alison had heard her father make that statement many times over the years. Her uncle had worked at the Davenport copper mine and there had been an accident resulting in his death. Although an investigation had cleared the mine of any blame and had stated it was just a tragic accident, her father believed the Davenports had used their money and influence to cover up the truth and that really there had been a serious lapse in safety standards.

Even though this had happened over forty years ago and the mine had long since closed, the bitterness in Alison's family was as strong as if it had happened yesterday.

To Alison's mind this had nothing to do with Luke Davenport. He couldn't change or help what had gone on in the past any more than she could. But she knew better than to argue this with her dad. His beloved brother was dead and that was all he could think of where the Davenports were concerned.

Six years after their first proper meeting she met up with Luke again. It was at a birthday party in London, a trendy affair in a wine bar down by the River Thames. Alison was edging towards the door, trying to escape the crush of people and the heat and noise, when she suddenly spotted him across the room. Even though it was several years since she had last seen him, she knew him instantly. There was no mistaking Luke Davenport; he was so attractive, tall and dark with a commanding presence that drew a woman's attention and held it.

She watched him for a moment, trying to work out who he was with, but there were so many people around him that it was an almost impossible task, so she made her way across to him.

She caught his eye as he turned and for a few seconds she could tell that he recognised her but couldn't place her.

'Hello, Luke; you're a long way from home.' Alison smiled and quite enjoyed the look of astonished recognition in his eyes as they swept over her.

'Heavens, it's Alison, isn't it...? Alison Trevelyan.' Along with the note of surprise there was a definite hint of male appreciation in his voice. He seemed to do a double take on her, noting the leather trousers that emphasised her small waist and long legs, and the sparkly halter-neck top she wore. The perusal was very far removed from the way he had looked at her the last time they had met. It was as if he was seeing her for the first time, noting the golden-red of her hair, which lay long and loose around her shoulders, and the soft curves of her body, registering her as a woman, not the gawky schoolgirl he had last encountered. 'I hardly recognised you. You look fabulous,' he said, and she felt a thrill of exhilaration unlike anything she had ever known.

'What are you doing up in London?' he asked.

'I'm at university; my flat is just around the corner from here. How about you?'

'I work for a company called Millington Hays. My office isn't far from here.'

'You're a high-flying executive, aren't you?'

'Assistant Director.'

'Sorry.' She grinned. 'The grapevine in Penray obviously isn't one hundred per cent accurate.'

'Thank heavens for that,' Luke agreed with a grin. 'How do you know Barbara?'

'Who...? Oh, Barbara, the girl whose birthday party

this is! Sorry.' Alison laughed. 'As you've probably just guessed, I don't really know her at all. She's the older sister of a friend of a friend. A whole crowd of us from university have dropped in on the spur of the moment...actually I feel like a gatecrasher because I hardly know anyone.'

'I don't know a lot of people here either. Barbara is a work colleague.' He smiled at her, the kind of smile that made her feel weak inside. 'Would you like a drink?'

Forgetting the fact that a moment ago the crowds had seemed unbearable, Alison accepted happily and followed him towards the small bar at the far side of the room.

It was hard to have a conversation because of the noise and the loud music and they had to stand very close, Luke leaning down to speak closer to her ear; the husky rasp of his voice and the feel of his breath against her sensitive skin set her pulses racing, and she was hardly able to concentrate on anything except the profound effect he was having on her senses.

Someone bumped into her and jerked her forward. Luke reached out a hand to steady her and for a second he held her close in the confined space.

The touch of his hand sent a thrill of excitement rushing through her, and as she looked up into the depths of his gorgeous eyes she was totally smitten...just as she had all those years ago as a teenager. She could hardly believe her luck that he was here now and that he was looking at her with equal interest.

He walked her home and they talked non-stop. There was this strange feeling of unity; she found herself opening up to him as if it were the most natural thing in the world, as if the divisions that had kept their families apart over the years had never existed.

She told him she was studying accountancy and they talked for a while about living in the city and the places they liked to go.

'But don't you miss Cornwall?' she sighed. 'I used to love getting up really early in the morning when I lived on the farm. Riding one of the horses across the fields towards the cliffs, breathing in the sea air, watching the fishing boats and just listening to the sound of the ocean pounding against the rocks. There is something magical about Cornwall, the way the mist and the light sparkle as a new day dawns. That feeling of peace and tranquillity…and belonging somewhere.'

As they stopped outside the house where she shared a flat with a fellow student she abruptly fell silent and looked up into his eyes with an acute feeling of shyness.

'I talk too much, don't I?' she said with a nervous laugh.

'No.' He smiled. 'I think you are quite enchanting, Alison Trevelyan.' The words were said so matter-of-factly that they sounded completely sincere rather than charming. Or maybe it was just the fact that Luke was so good-looking he could get away with any old line. According to the rumours back home, Luke was a womaniser, with one beautiful woman in his life after another.

'Bet you say that to all the girls,' she said, trying her best not to be thrilled by the compliment.

'Only the ones that I'd like to see more of,' he said, a teasing glint in his eye.

Before she could say anything to that he bent his head and kissed her. She would never forget that first kiss, the sensation of desire, of being overtaken totally by emotion and need. Luke was certainly a master at turning a woman on. When he pulled back from her she was breathless with longing.

'Can I see you again?' he whispered, and she nodded, unable to trust herself to speak.

There followed a whirlwind of dates, a time that was so exciting that Alison found herself living for the evenings or the weekends when she would see him.

He always arrived to pick her up in his convertible blue Jaguar and took her out to clubs and restaurants and long drives in the countryside. Everything about her time with him seemed so perfect, so idyllic. She felt as if she could talk to him about anything...and yet they always skirted around the feud between their families; it was like an unspoken pact between them, as if that problem was left behind in Cornwall and was therefore nothing to do with them.

A few weeks after they had started going out together Luke drove her down to Kent. It was a beautiful evening and the countryside was filled with the sounds and scents of summer, the sky a rich, warm blue. She had thought that they were going to a restaurant but Luke surprised her with a picnic. They had a most romantic evening, seated by the banks of a river in the warm spring air. The picnic hamper was from Harrods and filled with fabulous delicacies and Luke had even brought along a bottle of chilled champagne. Alison later remembered it all so vividly that she could almost smell the blossom in the air; she remembered lying on her back in the dappled shade of an apple tree, looking up at the blue of the sky thinking how wonderful life was and that this was just perfect...

'I'm driving down to Cornwall on Friday night, Ali, to see my father. Would you like to come with me?'

The casual invitation threw her, and suddenly made her face the fact that if she arrived back in the village with Luke in tow her father would find out she was seeing him…and there would be serious ructions. 'I don't think I can,' she refused.

'Why not? I'll be driving back to London on Sunday so you'll be in plenty of time for uni. I thought you'd like to go down and see your family for the weekend?'

'I would…but…'

'But you don't want to go with me?'

The matter-of-fact statement made her sit up. 'It's not that, Luke.' She felt herself going red as she said softly, 'It's just…why raise trouble? There isn't a lot of love lost in our home for a member of the Davenport family.'

Luke inclined his head. 'Tell me about it…' he drawled heavily. 'But it's time that feud business was forgotten.'

She smiled, happy that he felt the same way as she did. 'Yes…I agree. But if we arrive down there together they'll all know we're seeing each other and it will just awaken all the old animosities again… I'd rather not face all that unless…or until I have to.'

'If that's what you want.' Luke shrugged. 'But frankly I don't care much for subterfuge.'

'Yes, but it's easy for you to be unconcerned; you live in London, Luke.'

'So do you.'

'But only for the time being while I'm at uni.'

There was a small, strained silence for a moment before she continued swiftly, 'Anyway, maybe your father isn't quite as…'

'Dogmatic and domineering?' Luke supplied the words drily and they irritated her.

'I was going to say that maybe your father isn't as

angry about the past as mine is,' she corrected him quietly, her loyalty to her father suddenly rearing up. 'After
all, losing my uncle like that was a dreadful blow for
the whole family.'

'I'm sure it was,' Luke said softly. 'But it was a ter-
rible and tragic accident, Alison; it wasn't anyone's
fault. Your father's inability to accept that caused a lot
of further and unnecessary distress between our two families.'

Whatever else she had been going to say on the subject was abruptly cut off as Luke moved towards her and
rolled her gently back against the grass, pinning her beneath him.

'But that's all in the past, Alison. It's here and now
that matters.'

As his lips captured hers she forgot instantly what
they had even been arguing about. He held her hands
high over her head as his lips crushed hers and then as
she kissed him back heatedly he relaxed his hold and
they lay together in a heated blaze of an emotion that
had nothing to do with anger.

'Mmm, that was nice.' She stretched languidly beneath him, feeling like a cat that wanted to purr with
pleasure.

'Maybe a bit too nice,' he murmured, his eyes raking
over her upturned face with an intensity that made her
heart drum crazily against her chest. 'I've been trying to
be a gentleman and not come on too strong these last
few weeks.' His gaze lingered on the softness of her lips.
'But I'm finding it very difficult.'

'Maybe I don't want you to be a gentleman,' she said,
reaching up to kiss him again.

She trembled as the kiss deepened, delighting in the
touch of his hands against her body, feeling them as if

they were burning through the delicate material of her dress.

When Luke pulled back to ask huskily if they should go back to his place she didn't even hesitate in saying yes.

It was the first time she had ever been in Luke's apartment. She thought how ultra-modern it was with its panoramic views out across the docklands of London. She compared it with her basic lodgings and suddenly it struck her how far apart they really were in a lot of ways…she was just starting out, he was already a high achiever with a multinational firm.

But what really had made her nervous was the fact that while he was an experienced lover…she was a virgin.

'Would you like a drink?' He smiled at her as if he knew that she was apprehensive.

'Yes…thank you.' She watched as he poured them both a glass of wine.

'Here's to us,' he said lightly as he passed her the glass.

'Yes, to us.' She took a sip of the wine and then as she glanced up at him uncertainly he reached out and took the glass away from her, putting it down beside them on the table.

'Now, where were we…?' he murmured, a gleam of purpose in his eye that made desire and apprehension mix in a shivery way inside her. 'Oh, yes…I remember. You were telling me how much you didn't want me to behave like a gentleman…'

'Was I?' The seductive gleam in his voice and the heat of his eyes as they swept over her slender body made her temperature soar.

'So how do you want me to behave?' he murmured,

peppering small butterfly kisses over her face. 'Am I heading anywhere in the right direction?'

'Definitely…the…right…path.'

His kisses had always been hard to resist, but that evening as the darkness fell over London she knew that she wasn't going to pull back. She wanted him, had wanted him for weeks. As he started to undress her she helped him, her body urgently demanding her to get as close as she possibly could. When he swung her up into his arms and carried her through to the bedroom she was beyond any sensible, rational thought; all she wanted was to be next to him, to feel his hands hungrily against her body. Their kisses were so heated that her mouth was swollen from them, her breasts tight with need as he took off her bra. It was a wild coupling as weeks of desire and longing finally gave way and barriers came crashing down in a torrent of emotion.

Afterwards as she lay beside him, their naked bodies pressed close together, she didn't regret what they had done because it felt so right. But even then she didn't want to think too far ahead.

Luke didn't go to Cornwall that weekend; instead they spent it in bed, Luke teaching her the delights of love-making. He was a skilled and expert instructor and she was completely addicted, so much so that as the weeks passed in a glorious haze, Alison secretly longed to move in with Luke. But he didn't ask her and she refrained from making any hints.

At the time she told herself that it was sensible not to see each other too much as she had a lot of studying to do and exams still to take, but also she knew instinctively that Luke was a man who valued his freedom.

The day she took her final exam and knew that she had finished at university there were mixed emotions inside Alison. There was a part of her that wanted desperately to go home to Cornwall; she was a country girl at heart and although she had enjoyed her time in the city she knew it wasn't really the life she wanted.

However, Luke's life was in the city. He was ambitious...and he was rising fast within the company he worked for. She was under no illusion that if she wanted to be around him she would have to be the one to make the compromises. So she applied for a few jobs and while she waited for a full-time job she took two part-time ones so that she could afford to stay on in her flat.

On her last evening at Luke's apartment they made love and then, cuddling together in the deep comfort of his double bed, he broached the subject of the future, asking if she had heard anything from her job applications.

'I've got a couple of interviews next week.' She hesitated before adding quietly, 'But I'm starting to wonder if I should go back home.'

In honesty, she was testing the water, wondering if he would ask her not to go. But he didn't say anything like that, just asked if she missed her family or just Cornwall.

'Well...both, I suppose.' She rolled over to look at him. 'Don't you miss home?'

'I like Cornwall but I've got other things on my agenda at the moment. To be honest I'm thinking of leaving England altogether. I've been offered a posting to New York for a while.'

The statement took her so much by surprise that she lay there aware of her heart thundering against her chest as she waited to see if he'd ask her to go with him.

'It's a great opportunity for the future. The company are putting together a new Anglo-American venture and they want me on board.'

When she didn't say anything to that he continued firmly, 'It's just a plane ride away, Alison, and I feel—'

Whatever he was going to say was cut off by the shrill ring of the phone and Luke reached to answer it. 'It's for you,' he said, handing the receiver over. 'Your flatmate.'

She knew instantly there was something wrong; Sandra never phoned her at Luke's.

'Your brother has been on the phone, Alison.' There was a moment's hesitation. 'It's your parents—they have been involved in a car crash.'

Luke drove her through the night to reach the hospital. He offered to go in with her but she refused the offer, telling him she'd ring him later.

Garth met her in the corridor and one look at his face told her she was too late.

Grief-stricken, Alison threw herself into helping out at home. Her youngest brother Ian was just fifteen and she felt she needed to be there for him.

Luke came down just after the funeral and they met on the cliff path that ran along the side of their two properties.

'I'm really sorry about your parents,' he said gently. 'I know what you must be going through; I lost my mother ten years ago, and it was a very difficult and emotional time.'

The gentleness of his voice stirred her deeply. She looked up and met his eyes and felt as if he was reaching out to her in a way that made her feel suddenly warmly protected, cocooned…it was the strangest sensation, but at that moment she felt as if she would trust Luke Davenport with her very life. What did it matter that he hadn't told her he loved her? she asked herself. After all, they were only words…and maybe he wouldn't take that posting to New York?

She found herself talking more about things at home than she had ever done. The farm had been left equally between her and all three brothers but Garth wanted to sell.

'It's the last thing I want. I love the farm and I believe we should keep things as they are at least for a little while…Mum and Dad have only just died and it seems we will be selling in almost indecent haste. But I've been out-voted by my brothers, and business-wise I can understand where they're coming from. Garth is brimming with ideas for the old Cliff House. I've looked at the accounts with him and he's convinced me it would be a viable proposition.'

'That's the hotel further along the headland, isn't it?' Luke said cautiously. 'It's been up for sale for a long time.'

'Yes, they want a lot of money for it.' Alison nodded. 'But even if I don't go in with them the boys' share of the farm should almost cover it with an additional bank loan. I just wish I could keep the farmhouse and the stables. But everything will have to go.'

Luke heard the catch in her voice and saw the disquiet in her eyes. 'It's not good to be too attached to things, Alison,' he said quietly.

'You don't feel sentimental about your home?' she asked.

'Yes, of course I do, and as I'm the only son I suppose I'll take over the running of the estate one day.' Luke shook his head. 'But at the moment I prefer to look to the future rather than the past. I find it exciting to move on, explore pastures new.'

She experienced an ominous feeling of foreboding at

those words. 'Does that mean you've decided to take the posting to New York?'

They reached a bit of path that was uneven and slippery and he took hold of her hand. The thrill of his skin against hers sent goosebumps down her spine and made her remember the wild, heady nights in his arms and suddenly she was very afraid that she would never lie with him like that again.

'They don't need an answer for another couple of months,' he said and she had the distinct impression he didn't want to talk about it.

'Well, I guess I'm going to be stuck down here for a while anyway until we get everything sorted out.' She tried to sound OK about it all, as if she were content to let things lie.

'Do your brothers want you to run the hotel business with them as well as invest in it?'

'Well…Garth is pushing for that, but I haven't committed myself. I'll have to stay around for Ian for a while anyway so I think I'll just take it a step at a time.' She supposed what she was saying to him was that if he wanted her to go to New York with him she wasn't completely ruling it out for the future.

'It's good that you're around for your family for a while,' Luke said quietly. 'But don't let them put on you too much, Alison. You have your own life to live.'

'I suppose so… Listen, you won't tell anyone that we are going to sell the farm?' she asked suddenly.

'How the heck will you sell the place if no one knows it's up for sale?' Luke asked with amusement.

'Garth is putting the property in the hands of an agent in London.'

'Oh, I see…' Luke's voice was wry. 'You mean he'd

rather sell the land to the devil incarnate than risk the Davenport family buying it?'

She blushed a deep red. 'Well, you probably know that your father made an offer for some of our land a while ago and Dad turned him down flat. So out of respect for Dad's memory we thought it would be better to sell to someone from out of town. You know the situation, Luke...' she added softly.

'So your brothers are as steadfast on this old feud as your father was?' Luke shook his head with impatience.

'Things are a bit raw at the moment and they just want to do things the way Dad would have wanted,' Alison said soothingly. 'So I'd appreciate it if you didn't say anything to your father about any of this.'

When he didn't answer her immediately she grew anxious. 'Luke, promise me you won't say anything!'

He looked down at her and for the first time she saw anger darkening his eyes to midnight-blue.

'Don't worry, the precious Trevelyan secret will not be mistreated. Don't look at me like that.'

'Like what?'

'The way you're looking at me now. All innocent, provocative softness...you know you're driving me crazy.'

'Am I?' She was totally bemused by the sudden turn of the conversation.

'You know very well what I'm talking about,' he said, moving closer, and in that heartbeat of a moment as his eyes touched her lips she knew exactly what he was referring to. It was three weeks since they had slept together and the answering ache in her own body was instantaneous as he reached to kiss her.

'I don't want to talk about family feuds or sneak around snatching a few moments with you in secret. I want to kiss you, Alison…but you are so damn tied up with the past and so damn young…'

'I'm not that young,' she said quietly, lifting her eyes to his.

'You're twenty-two and I'm a man of thirty.'

'So?' She angled her head to look up at him defiantly. 'What's that to do with anything?'

'Well, for a start I'm your first serious boyfriend.' He grinned as he watched her discomfiture.

'I'll have you know I could have my pick of men,' she taunted him back. 'In fact, I've been lured to a concert by one next week…Todd Johnson—'

'Hey,' Luke cut across her softly. 'Just remember that you belong to me, Alison Trevelyan.' He growled the words with seductive, teasing warmth. 'Who is this interloper?'

'I'm joking,' she admitted with a smile. 'He's just a friend of Garth's…I said I'd even up the numbers on an outing—'

'Well, just make sure that's all it is,' he said possessively.

She was to remember that moment so clearly. The mellow warmth of the air and the pounding of the waves on the rocks beneath them, the way he looked at her, the way he reached out and touched her face with such tenderness before drawing her into his arms. As his lips met hers it was almost as if she was at one with the elements…the untamed force of the sea against the rocks echoed the wildness of her response, she tasted the sea spray on his lips, felt the thunder of her blood pounding through her veins as his hands caressed her body. Longing spiralled out of control right there and then. She wanted him so much.

'How about if I book us into an hotel?' Luke asked as his lips ground against hers.

'I can't, Luke, I'll be missed at home and…' She felt his hands caressing her breasts; felt him starting to un-button her white blouse.

'Maybe I can't wait for an hotel anyway,' he mur-mured seductively against her ear and she had allowed him to take her by the hand and lead her into the corn-field beside them.

She remembered the blue of the sky, the gold circle that surrounded them and the heat of their passion.

Even now, thinking about that moment, she was ashamed to feel the heat of desire rising in her again. How pathetic was that? she wondered angrily. She had allowed herself to hope that Luke had feelings for her, but it had just been sex to him and when it suited him he'd betrayed her.

The farm had been sold, but not to a Mr Delaney, as the family had believed, but to John Davenport, Luke's father. The deceit hadn't been discovered until after the contracts were signed and by that time it was too late. Garth's rage had been profoundly deep. And Alison had been devastated. She had found it hard to believe that Luke had let her down so badly.

As he was returning from the States where he'd been on business, she'd had to wait until the following morn-ing to be able to ask him about it. First thing she'd dialled his apartment in London.

A woman had answered, a woman with a sultry American accent. 'He's in the shower,' she drawled. 'But I'm his girlfriend. Can I give him a message?'

'His girlfriend?'

'Yes, Bianca Summers; who am I speaking to, please?'

Alison was so stunned that she put the phone down.

Her annoyance about the sale of her father's property faded into insignificance against the greater personal duplicity. Luke had a girlfriend and if she was at his apartment at seven o'clock in the morning it was hardly a platonic relationship! How long had Luke being seeing someone else?

The hurt and pain she felt was almost unbearable. She was in a state of shock.

'I don't know why you ever trusted Luke Davenport in the first place,' Garth growled when she confided in him. 'God alone knows what Dad would say! Especially as you've gone and lost our land to that family!'

'We didn't lose it; they paid a very good price for it,' Alison muttered. But she felt humiliated. And that feeling was compounded a couple of days later by a picture in the local newspaper. It showed Luke arriving at a charity ball in London with a stunningly beautiful woman on his arm. The caption read,

'There are rumours of wedding bells for Luke Davenport and Bianca Summers. Bianca is the daughter of millionaire Edward Summers, and she is Luke's counterpart with Millington Hays in New York.'

'Might have known she'd be the daughter of a millionaire,' Garth said, reading the article a little while later. 'Those people always stick together.'

And suddenly it had become abundantly clear why Luke had wanted to go to New York...why he hadn't thought twice about revealing her secret to his father...why he hadn't been down to see her in weeks. Their relationship had only ever been a fling to him and now he was settling down.

Alison had felt like a fool. She'd felt cheap and used and so angry. But she'd had too much pride to sit around moping about Luke and she had tried to get on with her life and forget him.

Todd Johnson had helped. He was Garth's friend and he had also been getting over a broken relationship. His friendship had made things easier…given her strength when she'd had to face Luke for the last time before he went to New York. Her mind skipped over that last painful meeting.

At least she had dealt with Luke and kept her dignity. It was after Luke left for New York that she had discovered she was carrying his child. That and the day ten months later when she had seen pictures of Luke's wedding had been the worst moments of her life.

But she was on her way up now…things were under control…she was damned if she was going to let Luke ruin her peace of mind now.

Her office door opened and she wasn't surprised when her younger brothers strolled in accompanied by Garth.

'What's this, a family get-together,' she said lightly, 'or a lynch mob?'

'This is no joking matter,' Garth said as he closed the door with quiet finality. 'Look, Alison, we are going to have to bite the bullet and work with Davenport…we have no alternative.'

'You mean I'm going to have to bite the bullet,' Alison grated angrily. She looked from Garth to her brothers, who looked slightly uncomfortable. But it was Ian, her youngest brother, who stood up for her.

'I think Alison's right and she shouldn't have to see Luke Davenport if she doesn't want to,' he said staunchly. 'We can do without him. If Dad were here he'd be horrified we were even thinking of getting involved with him.'

'Dad is dead, Ian,' Garth grated dismissively. 'And you're only just eighteen. What would you know about pressure and how difficult it is to start all over again if you lose everything?'

As he spoke Garth held Alison's gaze. 'My wife is expecting our first child any day…Michael is just getting engaged and is counting on his job here to pay his mortgage…not to mention the fact that your cottage as well as mine is tied up on this estate, Alison. If the hotel goes under we are all in trouble.'

'Well, maybe the hotel won't go under,' Alison said softly.

'No, it won't, not if we except Luke's offer…'

'So what is his offer?' Alison asked tightly.

'I told you this morning. He's interested in buying into the hotel; he wants to be an equal partner.'

'And what does he want in return?' Alison's voice was tremulous. 'Are you really so stupid you are willing to accept Luke Davenport at face value? Have you forgotten how he went behind our backs to buy Dad's property?'

'No, of course I haven't forgotten,' Garth said dismissively.

'Was it you who told Luke that Nathan is his child?'

Garth had the grace to flinch.

Alison's hands tightened into fists as they lay on the desk. 'You had no right to do that…'

'Maybe he had a right to know,' Garth said defensively. 'And anyway, it's given him a vested interest to see that our business does well—'

'You are such a hypocrite, Garth…you hate Luke Davenport.'

'Well, maybe that should remain in the past, maybe I'm big enough to admit I might have been wrong.' Garth held her eyes steadily. 'Ring Luke and ask him to come into the business with us, Alison. Please.'

'He's not interested in the business, Garth...can't you see, he's just using it as a lever to put pressure on me, because he's curious about Nathan?'

'I think we should give him the benefit of the doubt,' Garth said firmly.

Even as Alison was shaking her head, she was remembering Luke's ultimatum and wondering what choice she had.

Luke wanted contact with his child and she knew full well he would stop at nothing now to get him. But the question that was really disturbing her was, why?

'I've talked to him at length and I think he's genuine,' Garth said again as he met her eyes.

'And what about his wife?' Alison asked. 'How does she feel about Luke's sudden interest in our business...in my son?'

'Luke is divorced, Alison,' Garth told her quietly. 'He and Bianca have been apart almost a year.'

CHAPTER THREE

NATHAN was asleep in his cot and the only sounds in the cottage were the lashing of the rain against the windows and every now and then a fierce growl as thunder tore the sky.

It was the perfect night for the devil to be out on the prowl, Alison thought, her glance moving towards the window as lightning illuminated the shapes of the trees outside the window, the perfect night for Luke's visit.

She remembered the sound of triumph in his voice as he had answered her telephone call, the smug, self-satisfied note as he told her he would visit with pleasure that evening. 'Probably around eight,' he'd repeated smoothly.

She glanced at the clock on the sideboard. It was quarter past now; he was late. Was he late on purpose? she wondered, because it really was a kind of slow torture to wait like this, pacing around the small rooms of the cottage, tension rigid inside her.

Alison went across to the sideboard to pour a glass of wine and then changed her mind. She needed all of her faculties to face Luke Davenport. Instead she found herself checking her appearance in the mirror.

Her red-gold hair was pulled severely back from her face, and she wore jeans and a plain white T-shirt. There was no way she wanted Luke to think she had made any kind of an effort to look good for him, but now she wondered if that was a mistake. Maybe she needed some feminine wiles to keep a step ahead of whatever game it was he was playing. She felt sure Luke wasn't really interested in the hotel...no matter what Garth said so heatedly to the contrary.

She thought again about the news that Luke was divorced. From what Garth had said, she calculated the marriage had lasted less than eight short months. What had happened? she wondered. Was it a case of once a womaniser, always a womaniser?

The doorbell rang and she felt her heart pumping nervously as she moved across the room to answer it.

Luke was standing in the porch. He was wearing a long, dark raincoat over a suit, but she couldn't see his face properly because it was in shadow.

'You're late,' she said tersely.

A flash of lightning lit the sky, illuminating his features for just a second; they looked harsh and ruthless somehow. 'About two years too late, I would say,' he said quietly. 'But you know the old saying...better late than never.'

He brushed past her into the house and took off the sodden raincoat to hand it to her.

'I'm glad you reconsidered.'

'I haven't reconsidered anything,' she said quickly. 'I just thought...that we should talk.'

'Yeah, I just bet you did.' His voice was dry. 'Or rather the family did. Garth can be quite persuasive, can't he, when he puts his mind to it...a bit like your old man?'

'Just leave my family out of this, Luke. This is between you and me.'

'I don't think so.' Luke grated the words sardonically. 'I know from experience that you can't just deal with one Trevelyan, you have to take them all on collectively.'

'I mean it, Luke; your argument is with me, not them. And I know very well you have no more interest in our hotel than in the star-wars project. So I want you to stop filling Garth's head with rubbish and I want you to stay away from my brothers.'

'Still the same over-protective mother hen, I see.' His eyes moved over her as they had this morning in the library, taking in her shapely body as if he was weighing her up in some way. 'Just how far would you go to keep your siblings happy, I wonder?'

Something about the way he asked that question made her deeply uneasy, but she didn't back down and she didn't break her eye contact with him. 'I'd go as far as it takes, Luke,' she assured him with a cool confidence she was in reality far from feeling.

Instead of being rattled in any way Luke seemed to find her show of defiance amusing, and that made her more nervous. She turned away from him to hang his coat up behind the door; she had the horrible feeling that she had just said too much.

'Nice place you have here.' Luke moved away from her into the lounge, his gaze moving over the chintz furniture and the log fire that blazed in the stone grate.

Alison followed him into the room. Never had she felt so tense, so on edge; her every instinct was telling her that if she didn't tread very carefully she was going to be in deep, deep trouble. 'Would you like a drink?' She forced herself to be polite.

He turned from where he stood by the fire and looked directly at her. 'No. I'd like to see my son.'

She didn't answer him. Now that she knew Garth had told him the truth, was there any point continuing to deny that Nathan was his? The question had plagued her all day. She knew Luke well enough to know that he

wouldn't let this drop…if she continued to fight he
would insist on blood tests and that would achieve nothing except to confirm what Garth had already told him.
Maybe if she just admitted the truth it would take the
fire out of the situation and before long he'd get bored
and leave.

'Where is he, Alison?'

Alison felt as if a great lump had stuck in her throat.
She couldn't find her voice.

'Alison?'

'He's asleep upstairs.' Her voice was a fierce whisper.

As Luke moved towards the staircase Alison was suddenly galvanised into action, running to the base of the
staircase ahead of him. 'I don't want you to wake him…
it took him ages to get to sleep tonight and—'

'I'm surprised that you know how long it took him to
get to sleep,' Luke interrupted drily. 'From what I've
heard he spends most of his time with a child-minder,
because you are busy playing at hotels.' He brushed past
her.

'How dare you?' Alison was breathless with rage and
it was a moment before she realised that he was striding
ahead of her, up the stairs. 'I happen to be busy making
a living, not that it's any of your business.'

'That's where you are wrong. Actually it is very much
my business.' He paused at the top of the stairs.

There were only two bedrooms in the small cottage,
one at the front of the building and the other smaller one
at the back, tucked away under the eaves. Unerringly
Luke turned to the correct room and pushed open the
door.

A delicate blue night lamp lit the nursery; it played
over the creamy colours of the walls with their colourful
murals of Disney characters. As Luke approached the

cot and stared down at the sleeping child Alison found herself holding her breath.

Silently she went to the other side of the cot and looked in. Nathan was fast asleep; he had kicked the covers away and was lying on his back, looking incredibly cute in his teddy-bear pyjamas. His cheeks were rosy and his dark lashes long against the soft skin, his dark hair ruffled in a few baby curls.

'He's beautiful, Alison.'

The husky note of emotion in his voice took Alison aback. 'Yes, he is,' she agreed softly.

Alison looked across at Luke and was unprepared for the tumultuous emotions that flared inside her. He seemed so moved…so incredulously awestruck. She had never seen him like that before; he was always so in control and never fazed by anything. That a small child could rouse such powerful emotions in a grown man tore at her very soul.

'Are you OK?' she found herself asking him gently.

He looked up and their eyes met across the cot.

'What do you think?' His voice was raw. 'You should have told me about him, Alison…you had no right to keep him from me.'

'I didn't think you'd be interested.'

She moved towards the window and stood with her back to him, pretending to watch the storm outside. But in truth her mind was far away and she was remembering the day Nathan was born. 'Let's face it, what we had was just a fling…we'd both moved on.'

'This ceased to just be about you and me the day you discovered you were pregnant with our child.'

Unable to bear the tension in the room a moment longer, Alison turned and went downstairs. This time she did pour herself a glass of wine from the bottle on the sideboard. Then she stood with her back to the fire, listening to the rain lashing against the windows, trying desperately to gather her thoughts and be calm.

She wasn't going to feel guilty about not getting in contact with Luke. He had left her in no doubt that what they'd had was just a temporary relationship...so why should she have contacted him? She hadn't needed him.

A few days after the speculation of Luke and Bianca's engagement in the local newspaper the gossip had been rife in the village that he was coming home at the weekend and an official announcement would be made. As the gossip had come directly from someone who worked at the Davenport house, it had confirmed all of the suspicions Alison had.

Defiantly Alison had made her own announcement that she would be delighted to join her brothers in their new business venture and would be staying in Penray for the foreseeable future. And at the same time she had made an offer on this small fisherman's cottage by the cliffs.

Her brothers had been pleased and so had Todd. He'd asked her out to lunch so that they could celebrate. It was as the two of them had left the restaurant that Alison had seen Luke sitting in his car across the road. He was alone and she'd had the impression he was waiting for someone. As the railway station was only a little further down the road, she had presumed it was Bianca and that she would be arriving by train.

At that moment she had really wanted to hurt him the way he had hurt her and she had been grateful for Todd's arm around her and more than a little mollified by the way Luke's eyes had narrowed as he caught sight of them.

She didn't kid herself that he had been jealous—after

all, he'd had the beautiful Bianca—but it had helped restore some of her ego to let him know she wasn't sitting around moping.

And yet as well as those intense feelings of craving retribution, of wanting to tear down that smug and arrogant male ego…there had also been a part of her that had been so glad to see him. Glad when he'd got out of the car and crossed towards them.

'Hello, Alison.' His voice was cool and when she didn't reply he stared stonily at Todd. 'I'd like to speak to Alison on her own for a few minutes if you wouldn't mind.'

Not one to be easily ordered around, Todd stood his ground. And it wasn't until Alison asked him to wait in the car for her to join him that he conceded and walked away.

'So who the hell is he?' Luke drawled derisively as soon as Todd walked away.

'I don't think that's any of your business any more,' she said shakily. 'I'm surprised you're even bothering to ask.'

'Is it true that you are buying the old fisherman's cottage up by the cliffs?'

The question took her aback; she'd only just put in the offer that day! 'Yes, it is.'

'You haven't wasted much time, have you?'

Luke's cool disdain really rankled. 'I could say the same to you. You are nothing but a rat, Luke Davenport. My father was right about you. Not only did you go behind my back and steal our land—'

'I didn't steal it—you got a damn good price for it.'

'Is that your idea of an apology?' Anger rose even more sharply.

'I've no intention of apologising.' Luke replied furiously. 'The land would have been sold anyway and I thought I was doing you a favour in the long term.'

'Well, I don't want or need any favours from you.'

'I see.' He shrugged. 'Look, I'm going to New York next week and I want things to be straight between us before I leave because—'

'Well, good for you; I hope you'll be very happy there.' Her heart bounced crazily as she cut across him, unable to bear to hear him tell her he was marrying Bianca.

Luke's eyes narrowed. 'I can't talk to you while you are in this kind of mood—'

'Great, because I don't want to talk to you at all. What we've had together was pleasant…it broke the monotony of London, but I don't suppose I ever expected it to last.' She hesitated for a few moments before adding, 'It was obviously never really serious, was it?'

Maybe naïvely she hoped that he would argue that point, but he simply shrugged and his voice hardened. 'No, I don't suppose it was.'

Hearing that confirmation hurt so much and all she could think about then was getting away from him.

But he reached out and caught her arm before she could leave. 'So what is between you and this guy you are seeing?'

She looked up at him then, defiance shimmering in her eyes. 'Passion, Luke…wonderful, sizzling passion.'

She got a certain amount of pleasure knocking his male ego. And it helped her to walk away with dignity.

At least she hadn't cried…that crack in her composure had been saved for a few weeks after when she heard that Luke really had left for New York and at the same time had learnt that she was pregnant. Ten weeks pregnant, which meant it must have happened when the affair was at its height in London.

She had never felt more alone or more scared than she had done at that point.

But she had told herself that she didn't need him anyway.

And she hadn't needed him…OK, sometimes in the darkness and loneliness of the night she'd wondered and dreamed about how things could have been different if Luke had loved her. But they were just dreams… illusions. The reality was that she had meant nothing to him.

The reality was that less then twelve months later he had married Bianca.

She had coped alone with Nathan for these last couple of years and she had coped well. She was damned if she would let Luke ruin everything now. And she certainly wasn't going to feel guilty.

Alison glanced towards the stairway, wishing he would come down and they could bring this whole sorry episode to a close. He had probably only been up there for about twenty minutes but it felt like an eternity before he finally descended the staircase.

She waited for him to speak but he said nothing, just stood next to the sideboard looking across at her with an intensity in his gaze that made her want to flinch.

'Well, now you've seen him,' she said lightly. 'Are you satisfied?'

One dark eyebrow rose. 'What do you think?' he asked tightly, his voice laced with derision. 'Would you be satisfied with a few minutes with your son after missing two years of his life?'

'Oh, come on, Luke! Spare me the sanctimonious

speech, it doesn't cut any ice with me, I know you too well.'

'Really?' His voice sounded contemptuous.

'Yes, really.' She put her glass down on the mantelpiece. 'You've been off pursuing your life in New York. You wouldn't have stayed around here even if I had told you I was pregnant.'

'And who the hell do you think you are to play God with my life?' Luke asked furiously. 'Don't you think you should have had the decency to at least give me the choice as to whether or not I wanted to be involved in Nathan's upbringing?' His eyes narrowed on her. 'Or were you too busy thinking about revenge?'

He watched the flood of incriminating colour under her skin with a wry look of interest. 'I thought so,' he observed scornfully.

'I was thinking about nothing except what was good for Nathan and for me,' she said shakily but she knew her voice lacked any kind of conviction now.

Had she been motivated by revenge? she wondered suddenly. At the time she hadn't thought so. She hadn't got in contact with Luke because she had her pride and she didn't want him to think she needed him in any way. But had there also been a small part of her that had thought it would be her retribution, and that it served him right that he didn't know about his son?

She took a deep breath. 'Look, there is no point us arguing about the past.' Her voice was low and calm. 'If you want to see Nathan, then...I'm prepared to be reasonable...' She could almost feel the words sticking in her throat. She didn't want to be reasonable...she didn't want Luke anywhere in the vicinity...but she forced herself to continue. 'I suppose you will be re-

but I'm not going to go away and I'm not going to back down.'

'So how come you're so interested in playing at being a father to Nathan?' she asked suddenly, her eyes narrowing on the lean, handsome face.

'Do I have to have a reason to be interested in my own son? He's mine, Alison…and what's more he is the heir to the Davenport estate.'

'Oh, you mean you are playing power games?' She bit the words out contemptuously.

'As far as Nathan is concerned, this is about doing what's best for him,' Luke said, his voice low and steady. 'No matter how you want to argue the point, the fact remains that a boy needs his father.' His gaze moved towards her lips. 'And I've missed out on a hell of a lot because you chose to shut me out.'

Alison tried to hold herself still so as to show him she was not afraid of him, but he was very close to her. He reached out and touched a finger to her cheek, running it across the smooth skin in a gentle caress that was very much at odds with the harshness of his words.

'So where do we go from here?' she asked shakily. 'What exactly are your terms?'

'I just want to get to know my son without you fighting me every step of the way.' He drawled the words huskily. 'Like it or not, Alison, we have a mutual responsibility for a child…the least we can do is act like reasonable adults and be civil from here on in.'

Alison didn't answer. The way she was feeling at the moment she felt it would choke her to be civil.

'So, here is what we will do,' Luke continued on in the same dangerously…pleasant tone. 'I'll come up to the hotel tomorrow and you can greet me, show me around, make me a cup of coffee perhaps…we'll discuss a few business points to do with the Cliff House and I'll consider making a financial investment. Then in the afternoon you can give Jane some time off and I will take Nathan out.'

She opened her mouth to protest but he cut her off smoothly. 'You can come too if you like. After all, Nathan doesn't really know me so he might feel more comfortable if you're around.'

She didn't like this at all, but at least he wasn't going to try and take Nathan off without her.

He stopped and there was a long pause while he waited for her to say something. What she wanted to say was 'get lost', but under the circumstances she bit her tongue. 'I'll have to ask Garth if he'll cover at the hotel for me in the afternoon. We have a wedding party arriving and—'

'I'm sure Garth will be very well able to cope without you. In fact, I'm sure he'll be delighted.' Luke smiled as if the easy acquiescence pleased him and that really irritated her. He might have won this first battle, she told herself, but he sure as hell hadn't won the war.

'I'll go along with you, Luke,' she said tightly. 'But only so far.'

'Now you're spoiling things.' Luke leaned closer. 'We can do this the hard way or the easy way, Alison. It's up to you. If you don't want to meet me halfway then I'll have no option but to go directly to the courts.'

'You like to play rough, don't you, Luke?' she said in a low tone.

He smiled. 'On the contrary, I think I'm being extremely civilised... If and when the lawyers get involved then you'll know what playing rough is really like.'

CHAPTER FOUR

'SO THINGS went OK last night, then?'

'Garth, if you ask me that one more time I'm going to go out of my mind. It went as well as you'd imagine...OK?' Alison was standing at the office window looking out at the sweep of the hotel lawns that rolled down towards the sea. It was a perfect April morning, the sky a freshly washed blue after the storm last night. 'He was very angry,' she added quietly.

'I suppose that is to be expected. I'd be angry too if Sonia shut me out of our baby's life.'

'Yes, well, the difference is, Garth, that you are very much in love with Sonia and you want this baby,' Alison answered tightly. 'You've planned it, talked about it and you are a very solid couple...it's all very different from my circumstances.'

'Yes. There's no doubt about that. But we all have to swallow our pride now, Alison, for the sake of the business. And I think it's going to be OK.'

'So do I,' Alison said firmly. 'I was going through the accounts again last night after Luke left and I don't think we need him. I think we can sort out the problems on our own.'

'And how will we do that? The bank won't—'

'Nothing to do with the bank; I've had an idea. We can open up our gymnasium facilities to members of the public.'

There was silence for a moment. 'I don't think that would bring in enough revenue...would it?'

'I'm still working on the figures and there are a few things I need to sort out. But it might.'

Garth let his breath out in a sigh. 'I have to hand it to you, Alison. You don't like to give in without a fight, do you?'

'No, I don't, and I think we need to be very wary of Luke Davenport.' Alison saw the flash of red as Luke's car turned up the driveway from the road below. 'Anything could happen. Just because he's shown an interest in the hotel doesn't necessarily mean he'll follow through and commit himself financially. He could just be trying to get back at me for not telling him about Nathan.'

'He doesn't strike me as that kind of guy. Quite honestly, Alison, when we sat down and talked I found I quite liked him. It made me feel a bit guilty about the things I'd said in the past.'

'Oh, for heaven's sake, Garth. It's probably all just an act. His interest in Nathan will most likely be fleeting as well.'

'Well, if it makes you feel better, you look into the gymnasium angle. But at the same time I want you to give Luke a chance. See how things pan out.'

'Fine.' Alison's voice was tight with irritation. But she didn't argue further. She brushed a smoothing hand down over her pale blue skirt. 'Do I look OK?' she asked, turning to face her brother.

'You look great,' Garth said immediately, but he hardly glanced at her; he was riffling through the accounts laid out on the desk ready for Luke's arrival.

'Gee, thanks,' Alison muttered, but Garth didn't even hear her.

'Do you know what really puzzles me?' Alison asked suddenly.

'What?' Garth didn't glance up.

'What happened with Luke's marriage? It didn't last very long, did it?'

'Maybe they just couldn't get on. Or, if he's as keen for an heir to the Davenport estate as he's making out, maybe he suddenly discovered Bianca didn't want children,' Garth muttered.

Alison glanced sharply over at Garth. 'Did he tell you that when you had your friendly little chat about Nathan?'

'No, of course not.' Garth looked up and she could tell he wished he hadn't said that. 'I'm just surmising.'

'I just wish you hadn't told him about Nathan,' she sighed.

'I never meant to hurt you, Alison,' Garth said gently.

'I know.' Alison nodded. Garth had already apologised several times. And she couldn't remain angry with him; after all, he was stressed with the business and he had a new baby on the way...he was just trying in his own ham-fisted way to keep things together.

'I think everything will be OK.'

Alison wished she could be as certain. Still, the idea of opening the gym to the public was a good one so if she worked on that maybe she could at least keep Luke away from the business.

She glanced down again at her outfit and wondered suddenly if the skirt was too short?

As dawn broke this morning and the storm finally abated she had suddenly come to the conclusion that if she was to stay one step ahead of Luke she needed to employ every strategy...every line of defence she could possibly muster. So along with her business plan she had decided to use her feminine wiles as well.

Luke had liked her looks once...had been distracted

by her on more than a few occasions. OK, he hadn't been interested enough to want to wait around for her when she'd had to leave London. But maybe she could distract his attention and soften him up a little with a subtle flirtatious look. Hence her short blue suit.

The idea had seemed perfectly sensible last night, but this morning she was wondering if she had lost her marbles; it was probably the most ludicrous notion going. Like trying to attract the attention of a man-eating lion with a few chocolates.

There was a knock on the office door and Clare put her head around to say brightly, 'Mr Davenport is here.'

'Fine—send him in.' Garth rose from behind his desk, and Alison noticed that for all his confident talk Garth suddenly seemed to be as nervous as she felt.

As Luke stepped into the room Alison was struck by the contrast between the two men. Luke was at least a head taller and although at thirty-three he was only four years older than Garth he looked a lot younger and fitter than her brother. Compared to Garth, who was almost completely grey, there were only a few strands of grey in the dark thickness of Luke's hair. The dark suit sat well on his broad-shouldered, lithe frame. Everything about him spoke of confidence, and money, and he seemed to just ooze with sexuality.

'Good morning, Garth,' he said cheerfully before swinging his blue gaze in Alison's direction. 'Ali.'

She could almost imagine that she could feel his eyes burning into her as they swept over her appearance, and unlike Garth he missed nothing…not even the slight awkwardness in her eyes as she tried to smile back at him. 'Morning, Luke.'

'You look lovely this morning,' he said lightly.

'Thank you.' She looked away from him, acutely

aware that Luke was just acting, that his pleasant demeanour was most probably a thin veneer over total indifference.

'Make yourself comfortable, Luke.' Garth waved a hand towards one of the comfortable chairs in the office. 'I thought maybe we could go through some paperwork and discuss—'

'If you don't mind, Garth, I would prefer it if Alison would just give me a tour of the hotel this morning…bring me up to speed on exactly the state of your operation.' Although his voice was perfectly polite, there was a steely edge that told them both he intended to do things his way.

'Fine…whatever you'd like, Luke,' Garth said eagerly and Alison cringed at the gushing note in her brother's voice. She wanted to tell him to pull himself together, but instead stepped forward to take Luke's attention.

'Let's get the show on the road, then, shall we, Luke?' she said crisply.

'By all means,' he smiled.

Garth followed them towards the door and it was very obvious that he wanted to accompany them. 'Now, I think it would be better if we start over in the gymnasium and work our way back,' he said. 'I think you'll be impressed with our leisure facilities, Luke…its all brand-new, state-of-the-art—'

'Yes, I'm sure it is.' Luke reached for the door handle. 'We'll talk later, Garth.' Alison had a fleeting glimpse of her brother's worried expression before Luke firmly closed the door on him.

'You could have let him accompany us,' she said. 'I think he was looking forward to showing you around himself.'

'Well, I was looking forward to you showing me around,' Luke said.

His gaze moved to her legs as she walked ahead of him towards the reception area.

'This is the main reception area,' she said in a businesslike tone, stopping so that he could glance around.

Clare smiled at Luke as she turned and caught his eye.

'We've just upgraded the bookings systems on the computers and we're using the latest technology,' Alison swept on.

'Which programme are you running?' he asked with interest.

She answered him and then waited while he flicked through a few screens, looking at future bookings. Clare leaned forward to assist him, smiling at him with undisguised interest.

'So when you're ready...' Impatiently Alison moved away. 'The library is through there. You saw that yesterday.'

After a few moments and a polite word of thanks to Clare, Luke followed her.

'The main lounge is through that double door.' She walked across and opened the door, allowing him to look through to the pretty room with its pale buttercup-yellow carpets and eggshell-blue furnishings. Like the other public rooms it was empty.

'How many guests have you in the hotel at the moment?' Luke asked.

'About fifty.'

'So it's about, what...one quarter occupied?'

'Yes, but we are expecting a lot more guests this afternoon,' Alison told him hastily. She hated having to divulge just how quiet things had been. 'We have a wedding at the weekend. So people are starting to arrive for that.'

'Do you have a licence for people to get married here?'

Alison nodded and walked through the lounge to lead him out into a large Victorian conservatory. Although it was built in keeping with the era of the hotel it was completely modern with exquisite stained glass in some of the windows that looked out towards the sea. 'We use this room for wedding services.'

'Very romantic... I'll have to keep it in mind if I ever decide to tie the knot again.'

The casual remark made her look over towards him. 'Garth told me that you'd got divorced. I was surprised.'

'Penray grapevine didn't pick up on that news, I take it?' he asked sardonically.

She shook her head.

'Figures.' Luke shrugged. 'My father was pretty cut up about it. When I phoned and said I'd got some news, I think he was hoping it was news of a grandchild...not a divorce.' For a second Luke was silent before adding quietly, 'It was the hardest thing I ever had to tell him.'

Alison felt a sudden rush of sympathy at the sudden bleak expression in his eyes. 'I'm sorry, Luke.'

'We were just the wrong people for each other.' Luke shrugged. Then lightened his tone. 'But it hasn't put me off trying again.'

His reply sent alarm bells ringing in Alison's subconscious. If Luke was going to challenge her for custody of Nathan, as he had threatened last night, she presumed it could stand him in good stead to get himself a wife.

'Shall we walk outside for a while?' He moved past her to open the door out onto the terrace.

Although the sun was shining there was a cool April

breeze cutting in from the sea. Alison shivered as she followed Luke outside, but she wasn't sure if it was her thoughts that chilled her or the weather.

Luke wasn't going to get married just to get Nathan, she tried to reassure herself. He'd been bluffing last night when he said he might fight for custody. Just trying to worry her. She had no doubt that Luke wanted to get to know his son, but he wouldn't want to be tied down with him permanently; he was a bachelor at heart. You only had to look at his car to know that.

But even as she told herself this, Alison was remembering the expression on Luke's face as he'd looked into Nathan's cot last night...and the way he had talked just now about how his father had wanted a grandchild, and suddenly she wasn't so sure.

Luke was ahead of her on the long terrace but he stopped and waited for her.

'Well, it's all very pleasing on the eye,' he commented. Something about the way he said that and the way he was watching her made her acutely self-conscious. She wasn't sure if he was talking about her appearance or the hotel.

'Let me get this straight,' he said conversationally as she reached him. 'You and your three brothers all have an equal share in the business?'

'Yes, that right.' She had to force herself to answer that question politely. Having to discuss her family business with him was galling.

'And you and Garth manage the place between you?'

'Yes, but Michael and Ian also work here. Michael is the head chef and Ian is still at catering college, but works here some evenings and most weekends.'

'It must be pretty devastating for all of you, then, that you can't make the place pay.'

The ease with which he reflected on that fact really set her nerves on edge. 'The place was paying very well. We are just having some minor setbacks. But I have it all in hand.'

'Really?' Luke's voice was dry.

'Yes, really.'

'Garth doesn't seem to think it's all in hand.' His eyes moved over her, taking in the feisty way she was looking up at him. Alison had never been short of spirit, he thought. She was intelligent and articulate and very beautiful. He remembered the many lively debates they used to have in London, the way she always held her ground stubbornly, the way those conversations usually ended with them laughing and kissing, her fire spilling over into a passion as heated as her red hair.

'That's because he's panicking but I'm not,' she said confidently now. 'I know I can sort everything out.'

'Fine.' He nodded. 'So what are your plans?'

She opened her mouth to tell him and then thought better of it. 'Never mind my plans, what about your plans? You have no real intention of investing in the business, Luke, have you? This is all just an elaborate charade to get back at me.'

'Get back at you?' He repeated her words calmly and then said, 'You make me sound like a child in the playground who is angry because you've stolen his sweets. It's a little more serious than that, Alison.'

'But the issue of...our son...has nothing to do with the issue of this hotel. I think the two things should be kept separate.'

'I'm sure you do.' Luke shrugged. 'But I'm interested in the hotel anyway.' His eyes raked over the softness of her complexion. 'Very interested,' he added gently.

'Oh, come on, Luke! You've got big business interests

overseas; this place is too small for you to be genuinely attracted by it.'

'But I am attracted by it, Ali,' he said again, more firmly this time.

Like a shark sensing blood in the water, she thought nervously.

She remembered the worried look on Garth's face as they left the office…she thought about Michael, who would be getting married soon, and she took a deep breath. This was all getting out of hand and she needed to do something.

'Look, I can understand you being…shocked… finding out about Nathan the way you did,' she said quietly. 'But don't take it out on my brothers.'

When he didn't say anything she took a step closer to him and, trying to ignore the voices of caution, she raised a hand to rest it on the front of his jacket. 'We used to be close, Luke. You used to care about me once…'

'Yes, I did.' His eyes raked over her upturned face. He noticed the way her green-gold eyes were looking up at him so temptingly and the soft, provocative curve of her lips, sweet yet disturbingly vulnerable. 'I remember very well how I felt about you, Ali.'

'So how about if we call a truce…for old times' sake?'

It was surprisingly pleasant being this close to him, she thought suddenly. She remembered how wonderful his lips had once felt against hers. What would it be like to be kissed by him…just one more time?

Her senses took up the idea and urged her forward. Just a brief kiss, she told herself. What harm could it do? Nothing except perhaps put Luke off his guard. And it might help her prove to herself that she was definitely over him, that he held no more power over her senses.

'Luke?' Her voice was unconsciously husky and inviting.

She sensed his hesitation and then as she moistened her lips nervously he took her off guard and bent his head towards hers. She felt a flare of triumph as their lips met and then a blaze of longing so overwhelming that it took her totally by surprise and she could do nothing but melt against him.

Desire like a languid liquid heat spread through her body, making her feel weak. His lips were gentle at first and then as his arms wrapped around her, drawing her close against the hard, powerful body, his kiss became fiercely possessive.

He was the one to pull back from her and for a long moment all she could do was stare up into his eyes, completely dazed. So much for telling herself that she could move away from him after a brief kiss, that she would prove to herself that he no longer had any power over her senses! All she had done was prove the complete opposite.

'Well, that was a pleasant trip down memory lane...' His lips twisted ruefully and she wasn't sure if he was being sarcastic or not. There was an edge to his voice that she couldn't quite comprehend.

'I suppose it was.' She stepped further back from him. 'But it shouldn't have happened.' She cursed the fact that her voice was unsteady...and, worse still...uncertain.

'You're a good actress, I'll give you that, Alison.' His voice hardened.

'I beg your pardon?'

'You wanted me to kiss you. You sent out a clear invitation with those big, beautiful eyes…and I obliged.'

'I did no such thing!' she lied vehemently, trying desperately to salvage some pride.

But she could see just by the glint of dry humour in his eyes that he wasn't fooled for a minute.

She had made a complete fiasco of that, she thought, furious with herself. OK, she had wanted him to kiss her…but not *like that*. And she certainly hadn't been prepared for the resurgence of feelings she'd thought she had lost years ago. He still turned her on, she acknowledged bleakly. Could still exert the same old magic over her senses. It was a very scary discovery. 'Look, I just want us to call a truce.'

'Do you?' His voice was ominous. 'Or are you just playing games?'

'I'm not playing games.' She tried to make herself focus on what was at stake here and not the disturbing intensity of that kiss. 'I'm prepared to raise the white flag…' She injected a confident tone into her voice and angled her head determinedly. 'If you'll meet me halfway.'

He smiled and for a moment he was silent as he looked at her…really looked at her as if he could see beneath the clever use of her make-up and the pretence of self-assurance. The sharp, perceptive gaze unnerved her a lot, especially after the warmth of his kiss.

'You love your family very much, don't you, Alison?' he said finally and then he turned away from her. 'What's over there?' he asked, nodding across the gardens towards a walled area.

Alison followed his gaze with exasperation; she wanted a straight answer to her question, not this sudden switch back to the business of showing him around. 'It's the kitchen garden…we try to grow a lot of our own fresh produce,' she answered quickly and looked back at him. 'So, about our truce?'

'I'll think about it.' He moved away from her, striding across the lawns, so that Alison had to practically run to keep up with him.

She wanted to ask him how long he'd have to think about it, but one glance at the closed, set look of his features made her change her mind. She knew Luke well enough to know not to push her luck.

They made their way towards the kitchen gardens and Luke stopped by the entrance, surveying the neatly tended rows of vegetables and herbs. 'How many gardeners do you employ?' he asked.

What the hell had that to do with anything? Alison wondered with frustration. She didn't want to talk about gardening, she wanted to talk about the situation they were in. But she gritted her teeth and answered him. 'One full-time and two part-time.'

Luke smiled to himself as he heard the impatience in her tone. She was obviously ripe for compromise.

He thought about the way she had looked at him a few moments ago, the melting beauty of her eyes and that kiss… Trouble was, even though he knew very well that it was all an act, that she was using her femininity to try and get around him and soften him up…he also knew that he wasn't immune to her. Alison always had been able to get under his skin. She had the uncanny ability of being able to just look at him in a certain way and unsettle all his strong, level-headed plans. He'd known, for instance, when he met her at that party in London all those years ago, that she would be a disturbance to his free, independent spirit, but had he heeded his instincts? No.

He stopped and looked back towards the hotel. This was a good angle from which to view it, he realised as he ran a businesslike eye over the impressive Victorian structure. Out of the corner of his eye he noted the fact that Alison had sat down on a garden bench to wait for him. He tried not to notice that as she crossed her legs the short skirt lifted just a little higher.

Luke knew very well she was deliberately trying to sidetrack him so that she could get the conversation back to where she wanted it. She looked fantastic in that suit, he thought grimly, but little did she realise that she needn't have gone to so much trouble with her appearance—even if she'd been sitting there dressed in an old sack she'd be a distraction. He turned slightly so that she was out of his view and forced himself to concentrate on business for a little while.

The Cliff House was in an ideal location, graciously designed with style. And all the work they had done to improve it and modernise it had been carried out with great care and attention to detail so that even the new annexes were in keeping with the Victorian era and looked as if they had always been there. It was all very picturesque, the red bricks covered in climbing plants, the beautiful, rolling countryside behind it, the sea and the cliff walks in front.

Luke wasn't averse to the idea of investing in the place. He sensed that compared to his other investments the return wouldn't be very lucrative, but money wasn't really a motivation. As far as he was concerned there were much more important things to play for here.

He'd thought about Alison a lot while he was in the states. He'd even come back once with the intention of looking her up. Then he'd seen her from a distance; she had been pushing a pram and Todd had been walking next to her. He'd jumped to all the wrong conclusions and after the briefest of visits with his father he had headed straight back to New York. And soon after he'd married Bianca.

But for that chance encounter with Garth at the golf club a few days after his father's funeral he might have left without seeing her again. Then Garth had walked into the golf club and everything had changed. They had sat at opposite ends of a deserted bar for about ten minutes before Luke had asked, 'How's your sister?' trying to sound casual, when in fact the question had been burning inside him as soon as he saw the guy. He'd half expected Garth not to reply, but to his astonishment Garth had transferred himself over to sit next to him and for the next couple of hours the two men had held a very enlightening conversation.

Luke had been totally stunned when Garth told him he was a father. And then he'd been angry...furious, in fact, especially when, confronted, Alison still tried to keep the truth from him.

But now as he glanced over at her he realised that those emotions were shifting. Despite all Alison's tough, confident words there was a vulnerable look about her that tore at him...made all the heated words he had spoken yesterday absurd...in truth, now that his frame of mind had cooled he wanted to say it's all right, don't worry, I'll take care of everything, I won't let the business go under. But he didn't, because he knew she would hate to accept his help anyway. She was a true Trevelyan, stubborn, proud and totally infuriating.

'You've done a lot of work to this place in two and a half years,' he murmured almost to himself.

Alison, who had been sitting staring at his back, waiting for him to say something, answered almost without thinking, 'Yes, and taken out a lot of bank loans.'

'Is that the problem?' he asked, turning to face her.

She hesitated, wondering how much she should say, then shrugged. What the hell? Garth had the accounts out ready for him to look at, so he'd see for himself anyway. 'We've probably done too much too quickly,' she admitted. 'But the figures allowed for it...I'd done my sums and everything was on schedule and going well. Then the foot-and-mouth crisis hit the countryside and everything went badly adrift. It's really hit the business hard.'

'Well, that's more bad luck than bad management.'

'Who mentioned bad management?' She looked up at him defensively. 'The place has been very well-run.'

'Knowing what a perfectionist you are, I'm sure it has,' Luke said with a smile.

'Yes, well.' She shrugged, the defensiveness fading. 'That doesn't make me feel any better, especially as it's my brothers' livelihood as well as my own that's on the line. I do the accounts for the hotel...I should have been more cautious.' She looked over at Luke then. 'It's ironic isn't it? We're out of farming and yet we still got hit by foot-and-mouth.'

'Life can throw some unexpected punches,' Luke admitted. 'Do you enjoy running the hotel, Alison?' he asked suddenly.

The personal question took her by surprise. 'Considering I wasn't one hundred per cent sold on the idea when I went into it, you mean?' She smiled at him.

'You didn't want to sell your home, I remember that much,' he said drily.

'No, I didn't.' She took a deep breath, not wanting to delve that far back. 'But surprisingly I do enjoy the hotel. I suppose I feel I'm building something for the future.'

He walked back towards her. 'Garth told me that he couldn't have managed this place without you, that you've held everything together through very difficult circumstances.'

'Did he?' Alison shrugged. 'Well, we've all worked hard, not just me.' She was silent for a moment. 'And it's been a challenge; the thing I regret is not having more time with Nathan. Sometimes it's difficult being a working mum. There are days when I'd like to be able to cut myself in half.' She stopped talking suddenly, realising that she probably shouldn't have said that. If Luke was going to fight her for custody of Nathan he could use a statement like that against her. 'But of course I have lots of help,' she added quickly; 'Jane is brilliant and things run like clockwork at home.'

'Yes…all right, Alison, I get the idea,' Luke said caustically. 'Don't overdo it.'

'I'm not overdoing it. I'm just telling you in case you think Nathan isn't properly cared for…he is…he couldn't be better loved or cared for if I had all the money and time in the world to do it. And that crack you made last night about my being too busy playing hotels to pay attention to Nathan was totally wrong.'

'Yes. I was out of order saying that, Alison. I'm sorry.'

The apology took her by surprise. 'You are?' She looked up at him as if she had heard him wrong.

'Yes.' He smiled gently at her. 'I was angry and I suppose you were right when you said I was shocked by Garth's news. I'm only just starting to think straight again.'

The husky rasp of his voice sent a strange emotion trickling through her. 'Well, that's...understandable.'

He came and sat down on the bench next to her. 'I suppose you were shocked when you found out you were pregnant?'

'That's an understatement.' She smiled, but he sensed the smile hid a lot of pain. 'I was very frightened, Luke. It's quite awesome to discover you're going to be a parent.'

'I'm just starting to realise that. I felt a bit of that myself when I looked into that cot last night.'

Alison looked over at him and smiled tremulously. 'Yes...I noticed.'

Her eyes moved over the lean, handsome face and she wanted to reach out and touch him. The need was so sharp that she had to move away from him impatiently.

As Alison stood up she snagged her tights on the bench and felt the ladder run all the way from her knee upwards. 'Damn it all,' she muttered, bending down to investigate the damage.

Luke's gaze instinctively followed her hand. She had fantastic legs, he thought, and a fabulous figure for that matter. But now wasn't the time to be sidetracked by such things. 'I suppose we should get on,' he said, rising to his feet. 'I'll have a quick look around the kitchens and then we'll go and get Nathan.'

'Isn't it a bit early?' Alison asked anxiously. 'I told Jane we wouldn't be back until the afternoon and Garth might need me here because I'm the one who dealt with this wedding booking and—'

'I'm sure Garth can manage without you for once.' Luke's voice was uncompromising. 'But of course if you feel that he can't...I can always go around and see

Nathan on my own. I suppose as Jane is there it would
be—'

'No, it's OK…I'll come with you whenever you're
ready,' Alison cut across him quickly.

'Well, let's get on, then,' Luke replied.

Alison pulled a face behind his back as he turned towards the hotel. The man could be so damn maddening,
she thought. And yet for a moment as they had sat there
she had seen a glimpse of the man she had thought she
loved, the gentle and caring Luke. But that man didn't
exist, she told herself fiercely. He had never existed, had
always been a figment of her imagination.

'Where exactly are you thinking of taking Nathan this
afternoon, anyway?' she asked, hurrying to catch up with
him.

'I'm bringing him home, Alison.' Luke turned then
and met her eyes calmly. 'Back to the Davenport estate,
where he belongs.'

Alison opened her mouth to tell him that Nathan's
home was with her, and then changed her mind. She was
going to have to tread with extreme care through this
minefield, she told herself. 'Would you like me to bring
him over for you?' she asked instead. 'After all, my car
is a little more child-friendly than yours.' She managed
to insert sufficient derision into the words without going
over the top. His sports car might be perfect for his exciting bachelor lifestyle but it was not designed for a
family.

'I'll manage, thank you,' Luke said calmly. 'And I'm
aware that I will have to make a few changes to my
lifestyle to accommodate Nathan.'

But was he aware just how drastic the changes would
have to be? Alison wondered suddenly. It was all very

well deciding suddenly that he wanted to play at being a father…but in all honesty he didn't have the faintest idea just how hard being a parent really was.

Maybe what he needed was a small taste of reality?

CHAPTER FIVE

'CAN'T you stay for just a bit longer, Luke?' Garth asked. 'I want to go over some of these figures with you before I hand over the accounts.'

'No. If you don't mind I'd prefer to look at the accounts myself before we talk.' Luke patted Garth on the back in a businesslike yet friendly kind of way. 'Thanks for letting me look around. Don't worry, I won't take long to get back to you.'

'OK. Oh, and before I forget, my brother Michael is having an engagement party here next Sunday. It's going to be a big affair—we've got a band on and most of the village is coming. You'd be very welcome, if you are free?'

Alison shot her brother a wild look of disapproval but he ignored her.

'Next Sunday.' Luke thought about that for a moment. 'Yes, that would be fine; I'll look forward to it.'

'Great!' Garth smiled. 'See you soon, then.'

Luke glanced over at Alison, noticing the frown marring the smoothness of her complexion, and he smiled. 'I'll see you back at your cottage, then, Ali.'

'Yes.' Alison didn't immediately follow Luke as he headed out of the hotel.

'Why on earth did you invite him to Michael's party?'

'Because I thought it would be a nice gesture.'

'Don't be fooled by him, Garth. He can turn on the charm when it suits him.' Alison looked anxiously after Luke, who had already disappeared through the revolving glass doors. 'I've got to go; I want to be at the cottage when Luke gets there. I'll ring you later, OK?'

'OK...oh, Alison?'

She looked around at him.

'Todd has been on the phone for you. I said you'd ring him back later. I think he's a bit upset because he's learnt from someone that Luke is back in your life.'

'He's not back in my life.' Alison frowned.

'Well...he is in a way,' Garth said gently. 'Luke is part of Nathan's life now and therefore part of yours. You are going to have to accept that.'

Alison backed away. 'I've got to go, Garth. I'll phone Todd later.'

When Alison walked out of the hotel Luke's car was already pulling out of the car park.

With shaking hands she unlocked her own car, tossed her handbag on the passenger seat and headed after him.

On the short drive back to her cottage, Alison's mind was racing. And Garth's words kept repeating through her mind. 'Luke is part of Nathan's life now and therefore part of yours. You are going to have to accept that.'

She knew Garth was right. She was going to have to accept that things were never going to be the same again. Luke meeting Nathan this afternoon was the first step. And this first step and all that it entailed scared her; where would it all lead? she wondered grimly as she turned into the lane that led to her cottage.

Luke thought he could have anything he wanted...that money and power bought him everything, but it wouldn't buy Nathan. She was determined of that.

Her cottage came into view, its whitewashed walls gleaming in the sun. It was only small with a tiny garden that was now a riot of spring colour. Alison had always thought it perfectly adequate for her and Nathan; in fact, she had felt happy there. Now, seeing Luke's expensive red car parked outside on the grass verge, she suddenly wondered if a judge would deem Nathan better off at the impressive Davenport Hall. She shook off the feeling impatiently. The trappings of wealth were not the prime concern when bringing up a child; what mattered most was love and commitment and security.

However, Luke could be right about the fact that keeping his son a secret from him for so long could go against her.

She was relieved to see that Luke was waiting for her in his car. He climbed out as she pulled up. 'What took you so long?'

'I followed as quickly as I could. I don't know why you are in such a tearing hurry anyway,' she muttered. 'You know Garth wanted to talk to you. You could at least have waited and had a coffee with him before we left.'

'I think I've waited long enough to meet Nathan, don't you?' he asked quietly.

'You saw him last night.' She tried to remain businesslike.

'He was asleep. I'm looking forward to meeting him properly, Alison. Surely you can understand that?'

The question was so gently asked that she felt a flood of sudden empathy striking her from nowhere. How would she feel if the tables were turned and she had been the one shut out of Nathan's life all this time? The answer resounded in her very clearly; she would feel cheated, angry, and very distressed.

But Luke hadn't wanted her, she reminded herself sharply as she walked towards her front door. He'd dumped her, humiliated her, and left her with no option but to carry on without him and make the best of her situation.

Luke was standing so close behind her in the porch that she was aware of the scent of his aftershave blending with the honey-like fragrance of the yellow forsythia blossom beside the front door. And suddenly she was transported back to that spring three years ago when their affair had been so new and the world had felt like the most wonderful place.

She remembered lying looking up at a clear blue sky through the apple blossom; the way Luke had kissed her with such warmth and passion. If only he had really loved her, all this could have been so different.

'Are you OK?' Luke asked with gentle concern in his voice and she realised that her hand was trembling as she put the key in her front door.

She looked around and met the deep blue of his eyes, the heat of their earlier kiss instantly in her mind as her eyes drifted towards his lips. 'Yes…' She looked away, annoyed with herself. This was no time for regrets. 'Yes, of course I'm OK.'

But as she pushed the door open she knew she was lying. She was far from OK, and she suddenly realised that a big part of why she was dreading seeing father and son together was the poignancy of what might have been…

The sound of Nathan's laughter was the first thing they heard. Then the clatter of wheels on the stone floor as he appeared in the hallway sitting astride the small red plastic truck he liked so well, his little legs pedalling like fury to turn the wheels.

When he saw Alison his whole face lit up with delighted surprise.

'Hello, darling,' she said softly and immediately he

got up from the toy to toddle across towards her, a smile of such welcome on his face that it made her emotions catch. She scooped him up in her arms and held the warm body close in a bear-like hug.

Then she looked over and met Luke's eyes over the top of her son's dark hair. He was watching with a kind of silent scrutiny that made her extremely uncomfortable. Aware that his mother's attention was elsewhere, Nathan also turned around and looked at Luke with wide, curious eyes.

'Hello, little fellow.' Luke smiled at him. 'How are you?'

Shyly Nathan buried his head back against Alison. 'He's not very good around strangers,' Alison murmured.

Luke's eyes narrowed and she wondered suddenly if that remark had hurt? She hadn't honestly meant it to and she wished fervently that she could take it back. There was a painful silence and it was a relief when Jane suddenly appeared in the doorway from the kitchen.

'Hi, Alison. I didn't expect you home so early! My goodness, is that you, Luke Davenport?' She stopped and smiled, her plump, good-natured face slightly questioning as she looked from Alison to Luke. 'What a surprise; I never expected to see you here. How are you?'

'I'm fine, thank you, Jane.' Luke smiled warmly at her.

Alison was only half listening to the conversation. She was aware that Jane knew Luke; the woman had lived in the village all her life, so it would be impossible for her not to know him.

Nathan wriggled to get down out of her arms and she set him on the floor again. He went back across to his truck and got back on it to reverse and then pedal off into the lounge again at top speed.

Luke laughed as he watched him. 'How's that for a piece of driving?'

'He's a great little chap, isn't he?' Jane agreed fondly.

'He certainly is.'

Alison noticed the note of pride in Luke's voice and the absorbed way he followed him through to the lounge.

Jane smiled at Alison. 'Nathan seems to have gained himself another fan.'

'Yes.' Alison could hardly concentrate on what Jane was saying, she was so acutely conscious of the way Luke was studying their son.

'Nathan hasn't had his lunch yet,' Jane continued on. 'I was just about to make it.'

'I'll see to it; you get off and enjoy the rest of your day.'

'I will indeed.' Jane took off the apron that was tied loosely around her ample frame. 'Oh, and before I forget,' she said as she reached for her bag and her coat, 'you'd only just walked out of the door this morning when Todd phoned. And he phoned again a few moments ago; apparently Garth had told him you were taking the day off. He wants to know if you're free for dinner tonight.'

Luke turned around at those words and she caught the sardonic look in his eye.

'I'll ring him later. Thanks, Jane,' she said with embarrassment.

The woman nodded and with a cheery wave at Nathan and Luke she headed out the door.

'I'd heard that you were still seeing Todd,' Luke said as they were left alone. 'How does he feel about Nathan?'

'He's OK with him,' Alison answered hesitantly.

'Good.' Their eyes held for a moment too long then Nathan distracted them. He'd got his truck stuck between a side-table and a chair, and he was impatiently trying to push his way out.

'Hey! You'll never pass your driving test if you don't know the width of your vehicle,' Luke told him with an indulgent smile as he turned to help him out.

He didn't try to return to the conversation and Alison felt a pang of relief. She didn't want to discuss her friendship with Todd.

She sat down on the arm of one of the chairs and watched father and son for a few moments. It seemed so strange seeing them together. Their eyes were exactly the same beautiful shade of blue, their hair the same thick, dark texture. Come to think of it, Nathan had the same stubborn streak as his father as well...along with an identical winning smile. He was smiling at Luke now, delighted as Luke pushed him along for a few moments, steering him around the coffee-table, making the sound of an engine and then a horn as they narrowly missed Alison's feet.

'Very funny, guys,' Alison said with a grin as she sidestepped just in time.

Nathan thought the game hilariously funny. 'Again!' he shouted imperiously to Luke.

Alison smiled as she watched Luke patiently playing the game over again, pretending to miss her feet.

'I think I need danger money to sit here,' Alison declared after a few repeat performances. 'And your back will be broken, Luke.'

'Probably.' Luke said with a laugh as he pushed Nathan around again. 'But I'll worry about that tomorrow.'

The phone rang and Alison stood up reluctantly to go and answer it. 'Hi, it's me.' Todd's voice resounded in her ear. 'I've been trying to ring you all morning. What's happened to your mobile phone?'

'Oh... It's probably switched off; sorry, Todd. I've been busy.'

'Yes, so I hear. Why didn't you tell me that Luke had been in contact with you?'

'It only happened yesterday.' Alison turned her back on Luke as she caught his eye. 'Can I call you later, Todd? Now isn't really a good time.'

'Is he there now?'

'Yes.' Aware that Luke could probably hear her every word, she lowered her tone to a whisper. 'I'll tell you about it later.'

'Will you have dinner with me?'

'Not tonight, but—'

'Are you seeing him tonight?'

'Look, Todd, I can't talk about this right now but I'll ring you later.' Quickly she put the phone down before he could say anything else.

'Problems?' Luke asked as she turned.

'No, not really.'

Luke straightened and left Nathan to his own devices for a moment.

'I take it Todd's not too keen on my being here?'

The unerring accuracy of the remark made her blush.

'Well, I don't suppose I can blame him,' Luke said softly. His eyes were direct and unnerving as they held hers. 'I suppose he's got pretty close to you and Nathan over these last couple of years.'

'I suppose so.' Alison felt her chest tightening uncomfortably. 'He's a decent bloke, Luke.' She didn't know why she felt compelled to say that.

'So why haven't you married him, then?'

'That's really none of your business!' she replied, totally discomfited by the direct question.

Luke smiled coolly. 'You mean, he hasn't asked you?'

'No, I don't mean that!'

'So he has asked you?'

'I told you, Luke. It's none of your business.' Her cheeks were bright pink now.

'I think it is,' Luke replied coolly. 'After all, anything you do affects my son.'

Before she could make a reply to that Luke swiftly changed the subject. 'Anyway, I thought we'd have lunch at my place; let Nathan have his first look at his real home. We can discuss all this later.'

Alison wanted to say that there was nothing else to discuss and that *this* was Nathan's real home but something about the way Luke was watching her made her decide that now wasn't the time. So she just shrugged. 'OK. I'll just go and change my clothes.'

'You don't have to bother changing for me,' Luke murmured, his mood lightening with a teasing grin. 'I appreciate the outfit as it is.'

'Yes, well, I've snagged my tights so I need to change anyway,' she said hurriedly, heading for the door.

He damn well knew she'd gone to the effort of putting on a short skirt for him, Alison thought with embarrassment as she reached her bedroom and closed the door behind her. The damn man was so sharp he could cut himself. She really did need to try and cultivate more of an air of mystery around herself.

She pulled herself up short. What the hell was she thinking? All she needed was to think of a way to get rid of him.

However, as she opened her wardrobe and stared in

she knew that trying to get rid of him was not really an option. And even if it had been she wasn't sure if it would be what she wanted...not now.

The sound of Nathan's laughter drifted upstairs. They had looked so right together, she thought suddenly...father and son. Luke had been so lovely with him it had been almost a pleasure to watch them.

She flicked through the rack of clothes, angry with herself for thinking like that. Anyone could have patience and fun with a child for five minutes when the child was in a good mood. It was when they were crotchety and tired...and the five minutes stretched to hour upon hour—that was when you knew if someone was good around children.

When the going got tough Luke wouldn't want to know. He wouldn't have that much commitment in him, she reminded herself fiercely.

She took her hair out of the plait that held it back from her face, brushed it and left it loose. Then she slipped into a pair of faded denim jeans and a white angora jumper and studied her reflection in her dressing-table mirror. She looked very pale—you could tell she hadn't slept well last night—and there were shadows of anxiety in her wide green eyes. Reaching for her make-up, she put a brighter lipstick on and brushed a little more colour onto her cheeks, but it didn't make that much difference.

It didn't matter what she looked like anyhow, she thought, closing the drawer on her make-up with impatience. It seemed Luke wasn't going to be sidetracked from his mission and all she could do was try and point out to him that Nathan wasn't a toy you could amuse yourself with and then put back in the cupboard.

When she returned downstairs Nathan was sitting happily on Luke's knee as if he had known him all his life.

'Are you ready?' Luke looked up with a smile and then seemed to fasten on her appearance with such intense scrutiny that it made her acutely embarrassed. 'You remind me of someone,' he murmured.

'Do I?' She tried to sound detached, but she couldn't help asking curiously, 'Who?'

Luke smiled. 'A girl I met at a party in London.'

For a moment she was confused and then as she met his eyes she realised he was talking about the night they had first started going out together. He smiled as he saw the comprehension dawn on her face. 'You always did look incredibly sexy with your hair loose like that.'

'We don't have time for you to start talking rubbish,' she said crossly, trying to pretend an indifference that she just didn't feel. The truth was that as his voice lowered to that husky tone she could feel her pulses racing and her temperature rising. She turned away from him, feeling annoyed with herself. He was just teasing; he always did have a warped sense of humour, she reminded herself. 'I've just got to get a few things for Nathan, then we'll go.'

Luke stood up and carried Nathan out into the hallway, watching as she opened one of the cupboards out there.

He'd meant what he'd just said to her. She did have beautiful hair, he thought; the golden-auburn vivacity was a perfect contrast to the flawlessness of her skin. He remembered the silkiness of it brushing against his heated skin while they made love; he remembered the fire and the passion he had discovered in that desirable body.

His eyes moved lower over the tightness of the jeans

and sweater as he studied her intently. Alison had always been slightly on the skinny side but there was a new curvaceous quality about her figure these days that was very inviting. He suddenly thought how much he'd like to undress her, explore the changes.

With difficulty he tore his eyes away from her shapely rear as she bent to move some clutter in the cupboard out of her way.

'What are you doing?' he asked as she moved further in under the stairs.

'I told you. I'm getting Nathan's things together. I've got a spare baby seat in here for the car…ah, here it is!' As she spoke the item was pushed out into the hallway and next a fold-up high chair and a fold-up pushchair.

'Do we really need all this for a five-minute trip down the road?' Luke asked with some amusement.

She reappeared, dusting her jeans down, a look of determination in her eyes. 'Yes, we do,' she assured him firmly before disappearing towards the kitchen. 'You fit that lot into your car—I'll get his other things…oh, and Luke…' she turned in the doorway '…that baby seat needs to go into the front-passenger side of your sports car…sorry if it spoils the image.'

As Alison disappeared Luke smiled at Nathan, who seemed to be watching proceedings with a great deal of interest.

'Seems like Mummy is on a mission,' Luke whispered to Nathan. 'So we won't disappoint her.' He kissed the child before putting him down. 'You go find your truck and we'll put that in the car as well…OK?'

Nathan gave him a cheesy grin and then toddled off to the living room, looking all-important and busy in his blue denim dungarees.

When Alison reappeared from the kitchen Nathan was

standing on top of his truck on his tiptoes behind the front door, trying to watch Luke through the top window panels.

'Come away, sweetheart.' Alison scooped him up in her arms and was going to take him upstairs so that she could keep an eye on him. But he wriggled and cried to get down.

'Come on, Nathan, be good. You can't go outside...'

The child's wails grew louder as he pointed mutinously towards the door. Then magically the noise stopped as Luke reappeared.

'Anything else to go in the car?' he asked easily. He reached and took Nathan from her as the child leaned towards him with his arms outstretched.

'Just those bags.' Alison pointed to the small carrier bags with Nathan's lunch things. But her mind wasn't really on the amount of stuff she wanted to make a point of bringing. It was on the way Nathan was behaving...the way he had gone so easily to Luke astounded her. Where was her shy little boy? It usually took Nathan a while to adjust to strangers. He wasn't even this friendly with Todd and he'd known Todd since he was a babe in arms.

Luke picked up the bags. 'Follow me out when you're ready,' he said. 'I'll fasten Nathan into his seat.'

Alison watched as he carried the bags and the child outside. Watched with increasing incredulity as Nathan went happily into the strange car and allowed Luke to fasten him into his seat without a murmur. Usually Nathan made a hell of a fuss about being strapped in his car seat; he absolutely hated it.

She went back upstairs to pick up her handbag with a feeling of bewilderment. Honestly, children! They were naughty when you needed them to be good and good when you desperately wanted them to be naughty!

The drive to Luke's home was very short. In fact, the drive from the impressive wrought-iron gates at the entrance of his estate up to the house itself took longer than the journey along the public roads.

Alison was squashed into the tiny space at the back of the car behind Luke.

Every now and then Luke glanced at her in his rear-view mirror. She looked as if her mind was far away. He wondered what she was thinking about. Todd perhaps?

Every time Luke thought about Todd Johnson he felt a red mist rise inside him. The memory of their last meeting was indelibly imprinted on his mind. He'd heard the gossip in the village that she was investing in the hotel and buying the cottage because she was seriously involved with Todd. But he hadn't really believed it until he saw them arm in arm coming out of that restaurant, laughing and happy.

It had enraged him then and it still incensed him now, two and a half years down the line. And the thought of Todd being around his son...having a say in his son's life made the mist intensify even more.

He glanced in the mirror again at Alison and she looked up and met his eyes.

'It seems strange coming to your house for the first time,' she said softly.

'That damn feud has a lot to answer for,' Luke muttered.

'I suppose it does.'

The house came into view. She had never seen it before because it was so far back from the road and screened with trees; she had been prepared for the fact that Luke's home was a mansion, but the sheer scale of the place stunned her. It was a magnificent residence, the symbol of a mighty landowner's wealth and power. Twin towers were at either side of the building, giving the impression of a castle, and the huge front door was studded and looked forbiddingly unapproachable.

'I wonder what my father would think about my coming here?' Alison asked lightly.

'Well, if he'd any sense he'd think the visit was long overdue.' Luke pulled the car to a standstill. Then he turned to look at her. 'I should have insisted that you came down here with me that weekend when we were first dating. That damn feudal thing always exasperated me.'

'Me, too,' Alison admitted.

'So why did we allow ourselves to be influenced by it?'

The softly asked question made her heart turn over.

And suddenly the close confines of the car seemed too intimate.

'I don't know, Luke.' Her voice was huskily unsure. 'I guess circumstances just overtook us.'

She felt relieved when he turned away and got out of the car. He held out a hand to help her as she climbed out of the back; she tried not to take it, and then was forced to as she almost lost her balance. The touch of his skin against hers made her adrenalin rush. And when she tried to pull away from him he kept her hand firmly in his. 'I'm glad you're here, Ali,' he said gently.

CHAPTER SIX

ALISON jumped up from her comfortable chair as she witnessed Nathan almost knock a Ming vase off a side-table. Prudently she lifted it out of harm's way to put it on top of the fireplace.

'Be careful, Nathan,' she said quietly to the child. But Nathan wasn't taking a bit of notice; he was too busy enjoying himself riding around the room on his truck.

Alison returned to her seat and glanced at her watch. Nathan usually had an afternoon nap around now, yet he was showing no signs of fatigue.

They had just enjoyed a pleasant lunch served in the dining room by Luke's housekeeper, Mrs Jordan. Surprisingly it had been a relaxed affair, maybe because Nathan had taken up so much of their attention as he sat between them in his high chair. There had certainly been no awkward silences, in fact quite the opposite. A few times she had met Luke's eye and there had been almost a feeling of unity, their mistrust of each other simply forgotten as they agreed how wonderful Nathan was.

After lunch they had retired to the drawing room for coffee. And then Luke had been called away to the phone. He had been gone for almost half an hour now; she wondered who he was talking to for so long.

For a second her mind drifted back to the way he had held her hand as she got out of the car, the way he had looked at her. Had he meant it when he said he was glad she was here, or was he just spinning her a line with his usual charm?

She glanced around the room, admiring the rich turquoise and gold colour scheme, trying not to think too deeply about Luke's motivations.

The door opened and he returned. 'Sorry about that,' he said. 'It was a business call from New York.'

'That's OK.' She watched as he crossed towards her. He'd taken off the jacket of his suit and unfastened the top buttons of his blue shirt. He looked relaxed and extremely handsome. She wished she wasn't still attracted by his looks…but she was.

'What are you doing about your job in the States?' she asked casually, unable to resist the question.

'I'm going to be working from England for a while.' He sat on the arm of the settee opposite.

'Surely not because of Nathan?'

'Well, partly…I can hardly be a father to Nathan if I'm in New York, can I?' Luke said lightly. 'The project I was working on is more or less wrapped up now anyway, there are a few pieces to slot into place but I can do that from this end. Bianca is over in London at the moment so we will sort things out between us.'

The mention of Bianca's name made Alison tense. 'You're still working with her, then?'

'Just for a couple of months so we can finish the project together, then she goes back to New York.'

'It must be hard to have to work closely with someone you were once married to.'

'Actually, it's been surprisingly easy. The divorce was amicable and we've been able to remain friends.'

'I see.'

It all sounded very civilised. Could Luke ever be just good friends with such an attractive woman? Alison wondered.

She wanted to ask what had happened between them,

who had initiated the divorce, but she didn't want to sound as if she cared.

'So you'll be working from London from now on?'

'Some weeks I'll have to be in the city, yes, but I'm rescheduling things so I can work from home as well.'

Nathan bumped into one of the tables, causing a loud clatter.

'Nathan!' Alison sat forward in consternation. 'Go easy with that truck.'

Nathan grinned over at her and carried on.

'We should have left that at home,' Alison muttered.

'Why?' Luke watched the little boy with an indulgent smile. 'He's having a great time.'

'He's a toddler, Luke, and they can do a lot of damage with one little red truck. It doesn't matter at home because I've taken everything of value away but here—'

'He'll be fine,' Luke cut across her smoothly. 'This is Nathan's home…if he knocks a few things over it hardly matters in the grand scheme of things.'

She should have left the expensive-looking Ming vase where it was, Alison thought drily. Why she had moved it she didn't know, after all, this was supposed to be a learning curve for Luke. A taste of just how difficult young children could be.

'So you are not selling this house, then, I take it?' she asked as Luke turned his attention back to her.

'What makes you think I would sell the house?' Luke asked in surprise.

'Wasn't it you who said you had no time for the past, that you liked to move on? In fact, I distinctly remember you telling me when I said I was attached to our old homestead that it was a mistake to be sentimental.'

'Yes, I did. A house is just bricks and mortar. People are more important.'

'Really? I thought the Davenport motto was that land was all-important and that it didn't matter how it was acquired or who you had to hurt to get it.'

There was an uncomfortable silence filled only by Nathan noisily clattering over the polished wooden floor until he reached the thickness of the rugs again.

'Don't you think it's about time we put all those kind of squabbles behind us?'

She looked over at him, wrong-footed by the gentleness of his voice.

'You were the one to mention a truce this morning,' he continued softly. 'And I think you're right. We do need to put the past behind us and try very hard to make things right now for Nathan's sake.'

'Well…yes.' She nodded, somewhat relieved by his tone and by the agreement.

'So we're agreed, then? The white flag is being raised?' He grinned at her, that teasing grin that made her smile back.

'Fluttering in the breeze as we speak,' she agreed wryly.

'Good.' His eyes moved over her with a kind of tender assessment and she wondered what he was thinking about.

'So now we're on better terms, what about Nathan's name?'

'His name?' Alison shook her head, slightly nonplussed by the abrupt question. 'Nathan's name is Trevelyan, the same as mine.'

'On paper maybe.' Luke shrugged. 'But we can change it.' The suggestion was made quietly, yet firmly, and before Alison could say anything Luke stood up. 'Come on, I want to show you something.'

Nathan stopped what he was doing and looked over as Alison also got to her feet.

'Come on, Nathan.' Luke swung the child up in his arms as he headed out into the hallway.

Like the rest of the house, the enormous entrance hall was very impressive, with a huge curving staircase that came down from a galleried landing. The décor was one of graceful elegance. The antique furniture and ornaments exquisite.

Luke stopped by the foot of the stairs by a row of portraits. 'Now, that is your great-great-great grandfather,' he told Nathan as he pointed to the first painting of a rather austere-looking young man wearing black.

'And next to him your great-great-great grandmother.' Nathan seemed to be paying attention; in fact, his eyes were focused on the paintings as if he was greatly interested. But Alison knew this was for her benefit.

'Yes, all right, Luke, I get the point; I know your family go back for generations here and that there is a heritage for Nathan. But you haven't exactly been interested in taking over the family reins yourself until recently. You're still not really interested in the land; you employ a manager to look after the estate.'

Luke turned then. 'Yes, and that's my choice. Nathan will be given the same option himself one day. And even if he decides not to take it he should know that there is a strong bond that links him here and that bond is through his name…his real name.'

Alison was distracted as Nathan leaned his head against Luke's shoulder, his eyes starting to close, his arms curled up instinctively and comfortably around Luke's neck. And she felt a lump rise in her throat. The connection of the family name was secondary in

Alison's mind to the instinctive way that Nathan had bonded with his father. That was the real tie.

If she refused point-blank to change Nathan's name, would he hold it against her in later years? Alison wondered.

Luke watched the shadows in Alison's eyes, the indecision and consternation clear.

'I'll think about it,' she said softly.

'Thank you.'

'Don't thank me, because I haven't decided yet.' She took a deep breath. 'I'm not so sure that I want my son to have a different name to me.'

'It's pretty common in these days of divorce and remarriage,' Luke said wryly. 'And anyway, what about when you decide to get married?'

'I haven't thought that far ahead.'

'Well, if you're contemplating changing Nathan's name to your boyfriend's you can think again.'

'Honestly, Luke! Until someone actually proposes to me I hardly think that's an issue!' Alison pushed a hand through her hair unsteadily.

'So Todd hasn't proposed to you?'

'You've already asked me that once today.'

'And you didn't answer me.'

'That's because it's none of your business.' She was damned if she was going to tell Luke that Todd was just a friend, that there was no deep romance...especially as she had lied about it to him in the first place.

'But while we are on the subject I'm not so keen on the idea of you playing happy families with my son and some strange woman either. But that's all hypothetical, isn't it?' She carried on swiftly before he had a chance to remark on that. 'This situation is new to us both and all we can do is take it a step at a time.' Her eyes moved to Nathan, who was now fast asleep in his father's arms. 'At least we know that we've both got Nathan's best interests at heart and that's all that matters at the moment,' she finished huskily.

Luke glanced down at Nathan and, smiling, he moved to transfer him to his pushchair, which was sitting by the front door. Alison knelt to help him, fastening the safety belt around the small child so he couldn't fall.

Luke didn't straighten immediately but remained crouching beside her. He watched the concentration on her face as she secured Nathan and then tenderly tucked a blanket around him. And he was filled with a desire to reach out and sweep her hair back from her face, soothe the worried look away...pull her closer and feel the sweet softness of her lips against his again.

As if she felt his eyes on her, she turned and looked at him and for a second their faces were very close.

Luke could see the golden flecks in her green eyes and noted the thick length of her lashes, the creamy perfection of her skin, the soft vulnerability of her lips.

He wanted her...and, no matter how he tried to tell himself that he needed to take this situation slowly, that fact kept hitting him solidly like a punch from a heavyweight champion, knocking him off balance. From the moment he had set eyes on her again the feelings had been growing and they were remarkably familiar. Just like the old days, the sensuality that she seemed to exude was like a magnet. But now the stakes were so much higher.

'I suppose I should be going.' Her voice was a mere whisper, but the words seemed to release them both from a kind of paralysis that had held them trapped for a few helpless seconds.

They stood up. 'I think I'll walk,' Alison continued.

'It will give Nathan a chance to sleep and I can get some fresh air.' She pretended to look around the large hallway for her coat. In truth she wanted to get out of here as fast as she could. She felt acutely embarrassed by her thoughts a few seconds ago…wanting him to kiss her was wrong…she knew he had no real feelings for her and the lesson of this morning's kiss should stand as a dire warning.

She wasn't immune to Luke, but he was to her. Oh, sure, if she'd leaned closer he would have kissed her with expert and pleasurable ease; and if she'd been willing to go further he probably would make love to her. He was a predatory male and he enjoyed the thrill of a conquest, but there was no real feeling attached to the heat.

'Ali.' Luke caught hold of her arm as she made to turn away.

'What?' She swung to look at him uneasily.

'Don't rush off,' he said quietly. 'Come and sit with me in the lounge for a while.'

Alison hesitated. 'What's the point, Luke?' she murmured. 'I'm here so you can see Nathan, and he's asleep. I may as well go.'

'But I don't want you to go.' Luke's voice was teasingly provocative. 'I want you to stay so we can talk some more about my favourite subject.'

'What's that?'

'Why, Nathan, of course.'

Despite herself, Alison smiled.

'Come on.' Luke put a guiding hand at her back and before she knew what she was doing she was returning to the lounge with him. They left the door ajar so that they could hear Nathan if he woke and then Luke poured them a glass of wine from a bottle on the sideboard.

She sat back down on the settee and thought he would sit opposite her again, but instead he moved beside her.

She glanced over at him somewhat nervously and he smiled. 'You're right—we do need to take things a step at a time. Unfortunately patience has never been my strong suit.'

'That's the one thing you're going to need a lot of when you are dealing with a two-year-old,' she said lightly.

'When exactly is Nathan's birthday?'

'Three weeks' time; fifth of May.' She relaxed a little and took a sip of her wine.

'And have you got any plans for the big day?'

She grinned. 'Other than some kind of novelty children's birthday cake...no not really. He's a bit young for a disco, Luke.'

Luke laughed; it was a warm and pleasant sound and she found herself relaxing a bit more.

'You can come around and help him blow out his candles if you want,' she offered hesitantly.

'Thanks, I'd like that.' His eyes met with hers and he smiled. 'Listen...would you do me a favour?' he asked suddenly.

She took a sip of her wine and looked over at him warily.

'Will you look out some of your baby photographs of him so I can do a kind of quick catch-up?'

The question made something inside her twist painfully. What the hell had she done? she thought suddenly... She'd denied him nearly two whole years of his son's life... Guilt ate away at her and no matter how much she tried to tell herself that it wasn't her fault it suddenly sure as hell felt like it.

'Ali?' he prompted her softly.

'Yes…yes, of course I'll look out some photos.' She put her glass of wine down on the coffee-table. 'In fact, I think I might have a couple in my bag.'

As she reached to pick up her handbag he moved closer on the settee.

'Now, let's see.' She raked through the untidy contents of the bag, trying not to notice how close he was. She found her wallet and took it out. 'Here we are.' She opened it up and handed it across to him.

'Garth took the first picture,' she said, watching him as he opened up the wallet. 'Nathan was just two hours old there.'

Luke smiled, his whole concentration on the photo. 'He was a beautiful baby, wasn't he?'

'Well, I think so.' She grinned slightly. 'But then, of course, I'm biased.'

'No, he is. He's beautiful.' Luke peered closer. 'I think he's got your profile.'

'Do you?' She smiled. 'Well, he's definitely got your eyes.'

Luke flicked over to the next photo.

'That's his first birthday,' Alison said, leaning over to glance at it again. She smiled at the chocolate-smeared face grinning back at her. 'He'd just discovered chocolate buttons.'

Luke smiled and turned over to the third and last picture.

'That's the cleaned-up version of his first birthday,' Alison said. 'All traces of chocolate removed.'

'They're cute pictures.' Luke flicked back to have another look at the first one.

'You can keep them if you want,' Alison said with a shrug.

He looked over at her. 'Are you sure?'

She nodded. 'I've got others at home.'

'Thanks.' He smiled at her. The smile did very warm things to her inside. She watched as he put the photos down on the table. 'Alison, would you have dinner with me tomorrow night?'

The sudden question really took her aback. 'So we can discuss Nathan some more?' she asked cautiously.

He shook his head. 'No, so we can discuss what went wrong between us and where exactly we're going to go from here.'

She felt her heart slam against her chest. 'That sounds a bit heavy,' she said nervously. 'We know what went wrong between us. We had an affair and it didn't stand the test of being separated for even six weeks!'

'We both made mistakes, I'll grant you—'

'Yes, so let's just leave it at that.'

'We still need to discuss the future,' Luke said calmly.

'I think one day at a time is all I can think about right now.'

'OK, well, let's think about tomorrow. Will you have dinner with me? Please, Ali?' She started to shake her head. 'What's the matter, are you suddenly scared of me or something?'

'No! Of course not!' But even as she was denying that accusation she was wondering if it was true. There was a part of her that was scared of him...scared of how easily he was able to make her emotions rule her brain.

'So have dinner with me tomorrow. There's a new French restaurant opened at Grange. You used to love French food if I remember rightly?'

She was surprised he remembered that.

'How much can one meal in pleasant surroundings hurt?'

She wavered. Maybe it would be good to talk on neu-

tral territory. And he was Nathan's father—they did need
to be able to communicate.

Alison took a deep breath. 'OK,' she nodded, 'dinner
would be nice.'

He leaned closer and too late she realised he intended
to kiss her. Before she could move or even think his lips
were on hers, masterfully and sweetly seductive. Then
he drew back.

'What was that for?' she asked, her breathing uneven
and her mind clouded with confusing and conflicting
thoughts.

'Just sealing the deal.' He smiled at her.

CHAPTER SEVEN

'DINNER would be nice!' Alison mocked herself again and again as she stepped out of the shower and dried herself. What the hell had she been thinking about?

Dinner with Luke would be anything but nice; it would be a complete nightmare. Once they had exhausted the subject of Nathan, what would they talk about? She wrapped herself in a bath towel and padded through to her bedroom to get ready. She flicked through the rows of clothing in her wardrobe, searching for her little black dress.

It would be like dining with the devil. She had tried to phone him up today to cancel, but the phone had rung and rung and no one had answered. Which was weird, considering he had a housekeeper. She'd thought she would at least be able to leave a message.

To add to the dilemma, when she had arrived home from work Jane had informed her that Luke had been at the house. That she had made him a sandwich and coffee and he had played with Nathan for about an hour.

Jane must be wondering what was going on, especially as she was coming over to babysit for her tonight. Luke's two trips to the house in twenty-four hours would certainly have started the tongues wagging in the village. For that reason she had phoned Todd to tell him what was going on. She didn't want him hearing from someone else that she was seeing Luke tonight.

He hadn't been too pleased but there wasn't a lot he could say. Even though they didn't have a romantic relationship she had felt awkward about the situation, especially as she couldn't really explain it. She'd tried to just shrug it off as a meeting to discuss Nathan... Todd had merely grunted.

Alison sat down at the dressing-table and dried her hair. Then she applied a light make-up and slipped into the black dress. It was stylish without being overly stated.

For a moment she studied her reflection. She remembered the first time she'd gone out with Luke on a date; she remembered the butterflies of excitement and anticipation. It wasn't so different from the feelings that were inside her now. The thought made her frown. Back then she had been naïve and stupid. She was older and wiser now and she'd learnt her lesson; Luke wasn't to be trusted. This wasn't a date, she reminded herself as she went downstairs—this was business.

Yet the memories of his kiss continued to tease her provocatively. What kind of game was Luke playing? she wondered.

Jane arrived exactly on time, followed a few minutes later by Luke. When she opened the door to him she was glad she had made the effort to dress smartly because he looked spectacular in a pale grey suit.

'Hi.' He smiled and his eyes flicked over her slender figure admiringly. 'You look lovely.'

'Thanks.' She tried very hard to ignore the tingle of awareness that stirred inside her as he brushed past her into the hall.

'How's Nathan?' he asked.

'Fast asleep in his cot...do you want to go up and have a look at him?'

'No. I'll see him when we get back.'

Did that mean he expected her to invite him in when

they returned? She had been telling herself it would just
be a quick meal and then she would say goodnight.

'I don't want to be too late tonight, Luke,' she said
quickly.

'Busy day tomorrow?'

'Yes, I have to be up bright and early.' Her words
were firm and probably unnecessarily defensive. But she
didn't want him to get the wrong idea. Yes, she had
agreed to dinner and suggested a truce...but that didn't
mean she was about to let her guard slip around him.

As she reached to get her cashmere shawl from the
hallstand, where she had left it ready, he took it from
her and draped it around her shoulders. The touch of his
fingers as they accidentally brushed against her bare skin
set her senses immediately on high alert.

'Thanks.' She picked up her handbag. 'I'll just say
goodnight to Jane.'

But Jane appeared in the hallway before they could
move. 'Have a nice evening,' she said politely, her gaze
moving speculatively between them.

'We will, Jane, thanks,' Luke murmured, steering
Alison out of the door.

'I think she's wondering what's going on,' Alison said
uneasily. 'I should have told her it was just a business
dinner to do with the hotel...or something...'

'What, and ruin her day of pleasurable gossiping in
the village tomorrow?' Luke smiled. 'Don't be such a
spoilsport, Alison.'

He opened the passenger door of his sports car and
waited until she had got in before closing it and heading
around to get into the car himself.

She'd forgotten what lovely manners Luke had, she

thought. Forgotten how easily he was able to make a woman feel special.

The powerful car cut slowly down the narrow lanes, the headlights highlighting the high hedges at either side of the road and the daffodils that nodded heavy golden heads at the edge of the verge.

It felt so strange to be going out with Luke again like this. She remembered the evenings they'd shared in London…the trips to the countryside because he knew how much she had missed home. She remembered him parking on a lonely country lane one night and turning to take her into his arms…and the heat of their passion.

She cleared her throat nervously, telling herself not to think about things like that. That part of her life with Luke was finished. 'I tried to phone you today,' she said. 'But there was no answer.'

'I was out most of the day.'

'I was surprised Mrs Jordan didn't answer, or that you haven't got an answer machine.'

'I do have an answer machine but it's usually turned off when Kay Jordan is about…she mustn't have heard the phone.' He glanced over at her. 'What did you want to say to me?'

'Well…' She hesitated. 'I was going to say that going out tonight might not be such a good idea.'

'Why? Was Todd trying to put his foot down?' Luke asked sardonically.

'No, he was not!' She almost went on to say that Todd wouldn't dream of such a thing because they didn't have that kind of relationship and then thought better of the comment. Maybe it was safer if Luke believed her relationship with Todd was more serious than it was. At least it allowed him to consider the possibility that he couldn't have everything all his own way and that she wasn't going to be a walk-over as far as Nathan was concerned.

'Anyway, it's a good job that Kay didn't hear the phone, because I think going out together tonight is an excellent idea,' Luke said matter-of-factly. 'For Nathan's sake we need to establish a good relationship.'

'I suppose so.'

'Actually you could have phoned me at your cottage. I spent an hour there with Nathan this afternoon—did Jane tell you?'

'Yes, of course. And if I'd known you were there I would have phoned.'

Luke ignored that. 'Jane made me some lunch. It was very pleasant.'

'I wonder if she has already put two and two together and guessed that Nathan is yours,' Alison murmured. 'Seeing you together, she could hardly fail to spot the similarities.'

'Well, everyone will know the truth soon, Alison. I'm not about to sneak around playing the secret father.'

'I realise that—'

'I'm surprised you've been able to keep the truth from everyone for so long, quite frankly,' Luke said coolly.

'Well, let's face it, Luke, with our family history no one would ever have suspected that we'd…get together.'

'So who exactly have you let in on your secret anyway…just your brothers?'

She nodded. 'And Todd, of course.'

'Of course,' Luke said drily. 'Well, the whole world will know soon. I'm very proud of Nathan and I'm going to be shouting it from the rooftops.'

Alison felt the spiral of nerves inside her tighten even more. She wanted to tell him that they needed to take things slowly. But one glance over at the grim look of determination on Luke's face made her remain silent. He probably thought he'd missed out enough on Nathan, that he didn't have time to take things slowly. And maybe he was right.

They arrived in the small village of Grange and parked outside the ivy-clad restaurant that was the old converted mill house. 'I hope the food is going to be OK here. I haven't actually tried it myself, it's just been recommended.'

'I'm sure it will be fine,' Alison said, although secretly she wondered if she would be able to eat anything. She felt tremendously on edge.

Once they were inside the restaurant, however, and seated at a candlelit private booth Alison did start to relax, maybe due to the fact that Luke steered the conversation away from everything personal and instead talked for a while about what it had been like to work in New York.

He was very good company, Alison reflected as the conversation paused whilst their first course was served. She remembered suddenly how life had seemed exciting and fun when he was around.

As the waiter withdrew she prompted him into finishing the anecdote he had been telling her before they were interrupted. 'So what happened to this stray dog you found?' she asked.

'Turned out Fred wasn't a stray, and he wasn't an ordinary dog. He was an actor.'

'An actor?'

'Oh, yes, he'd been offered a part as a police dog in a movie being shot in New York and his owner...who incidentally happened to be the concierge of my building, had put him on a strict diet. So every morning Fred would eat his cereal or whatever he was supposed to be eating and then take himself off up to me for a slap-up feed. After he'd eaten he'd scratch at the door and as soon as I opened it bolt out and disappear. The concierge couldn't understand why his dog wasn't losing weight and I couldn't work out where this animal was coming from every day. He'd look all pitiful and pathetic as well when he came and sat outside my door. Turned out he was going out into his little back yard where the concierge let him run and was rolling in the garden, getting himself all bedraggled before sneaking up to see me.'

Alison laughed.

'Yep, daft guy here fell for it hook, line and sinker. The concierge wasn't impressed when he found out, accused me of ruining Fred's acting career! I said, ruin it? What are you talking about? The dog could get an Oscar! He cost me a fortune in biscuits and best prime steak.'

The indignation in Luke's tone made Alison giggle.

Luke smiled and leaned across and topped up her glass of wine. 'It's nice hearing you laugh, Ali,' he said softly.

The abrupt change of tone stilled her laughter, and for a moment there was a strangely loaded silence. She felt her heart starting to speed up as she looked across and met his eyes.

'So, do you think you're going to miss living in the States?' she asked lightly. But what she was really curious about was his failed marriage, would he miss Bianca?

'I think there will be stronger compensations being at home,' he said huskily, his eyes never leaving hers.

She looked away from him and reached for her drink. 'And what about you and Bianca?' she asked casually.

'We're divorced, Alison.'

'But you are still friends.'

'Yes, we get along fine...we should just never have got married. In fact, she's off to Hong Kong when our project is finished. She's had an exciting offer from another company.'

'Was that the reason your marriage didn't work out? She wasn't ready to settle down?'

He hesitated. 'The fault didn't just lie with Bianca.'

'You mean you weren't ready to settle down either?'

'I mean we were just the wrong people for each other...we didn't see that until it was too late.'

Alison took another sip of her wine. She sensed he really didn't want to talk about this. 'Well, it's none of my business,' she said quickly, appalled at herself for asking such intensely personal questions. 'I'm sorry, I shouldn't have asked.'

'No, it's OK. It's just not an easy subject to talk about. I'm still fond of Bianca; I'm just glad we were able to remain friends.'

She looked across at him. Was he still in love with her? she wondered suddenly and was surprised by how much that surmise hurt.

'Anyway, that's enough about me. Let's talk about you,' Luke said firmly. 'Tell me about Nathan. Did you have a difficult pregnancy?'

Alison shook her head. 'No, it was pretty straightforward all in all, which was just as well because I was very busy. As you know, we were setting up the business at the hotel and it was a hectic time. The Cliff House needed a lot of work doing to it just to get it up and running and we couldn't afford for it to sit around empty for too long, so it was a case of all hands to the pump. I was helping with the decorating as well as shopping around for what we needed.'

'You weren't going up ladders or anything?' Luke asked, horrified. 'I've got this vision of you nine months pregnant, painting the ceiling.'

Alison grimaced and laughed. 'What a horrible vision! No, I didn't do any decorating at nine months but I worked for as long as I could. In all honesty, I quite enjoyed being busy; it helped...' She nearly said 'take my mind off things' and then changed it hastily. 'It helped to speed the time along.'

'I should have been there,' Luke said gently.

'What, to do a spot of decorating?' She made light of the comment.

'No, to help you.' His eyes were serious now.

'I didn't need your help, Luke.'

'Todd stepped into the gap, did he?' Luke asked brusquely.

'Todd was a good friend to me but I never saw him as a surrogate father for Nathan, if that's what you mean.' She met his eyes directly. 'I managed very well on my own, Luke. I didn't need anyone else.'

Luke watched the candlelight flicker over her face, noticed the way she had angled her chin up slightly. Even if she had needed help she would never have ad-mitted to it, he thought. He knew her well enough for that.

'I wish you had told me you were pregnant before you left London,' he said quietly.

'I didn't know,' she admitted. 'And I didn't find out until much later. I was so distressed by Mum and Dad's death and...I just thought I was suffering from stress.'

She coloured with embarrassment as she met his eyes. 'I know it sounds stupid—'

'It doesn't sound stupid,' he cut across her gently.

'You went through a tough time. So how far along with the pregnancy were you when you found out?'

'Ten weeks.'

'Was that before I left for New York?'

'No, after.'

'I see.' Luke was silent for a moment. 'I'd assumed you knew the last time we saw each other.'

The memory of that scene flicked through Alison's mind with disquieting clarity. Luke's face, dark with annoyance, and the way she had secretly ached to go into his arms, for him to just tell her he loved her.

'Maybe it's just as well I didn't know then,' she said cautiously. 'It was all over between us, Luke, and you were leaving anyway. You wanted to be in New York and—'

'Alison, maybe you didn't need my help, but I would have liked to be around to offer some,' he cut across her firmly.

Her hand was resting on the table and he reached out and covered it gently with his. The contact sent a wave of longing spreading and engulfing her entire body. 'I would never have left if I'd known…never have abandoned you.'

There had been many times when she had wished he'd been around as well. The most poignant being the night she had given birth to Nathan.

She forced herself to pull her hand away from his. Luke hadn't loved her. That was why she had been in that delivery room without him and she shouldn't forget that. 'I didn't need your charity, Luke.'

'I'm not talking about charity, I'm talking about supporting you and my child.'

She looked across at him and for a moment there was a raw silence. OK, he hadn't loved her but he did genuinely seem to care about Nathan and that was what was at stake here, she reminded herself. Just because he hadn't wanted *her*, didn't mean he wouldn't make a good father. Making that assumption might have been a grave mistake on her part in the first place, she now realised.

'I did think about ringing you a few times.' She admitted the words in a low tone. 'But I honestly didn't think you'd be interested. And then when you got married I thought it best to definitely let matters rest.'

She watched his eyes darken slightly and took a deep breath. 'Anyway, I have given the situation some thought and I won't fight you over access to Nathan. I realise you've got a lot of catching-up to do with him, so I'm prepared to be reasonable.'

She looked over, trying to read the enigmatic features, but they had a closed, cool look and it was impossible to tell what he might be thinking.

'So what do you consider reasonable access?' Luke asked quietly.

She shrugged. 'You can see him whenever you want. But he lives with me.'

Luke smiled coolly at that.

'You don't agree that's reasonable?' she asked nervously.

'Let's say it falls short of my ideal.'

'Well, I suppose we're both going to have to compromise, aren't we, Luke? And, being realistic, you have your work to think about. You'll be backwards and forwards from London and New York probably.'

'I won't be going to New York that often,' Luke said firmly.

The waiter came and cleared away their dishes and placed their main meal in front of them.

'What do you think of the food in here?' Luke asked once they were alone again.

'It's very good.' She smiled, glad that he had changed the subject. 'But you know you didn't need to go to the trouble of taking me out; we agreed to a truce and—'

'I wanted to take you out.' Luke cut across her abruptly. 'There's no effort involved in it.'

The way he was looking at her made her senses fly into wild disarray.

'Do you remember that restaurant we used to go to a lot in London, the Waterside?'

'Yes. Of course I remember.' She looked away from the intensity of his gaze. 'We had some good evenings there.'

'I was in London a couple of weeks ago on business and decided to pay it a visit. It's completely changed. You wouldn't recognise the place.'

'I suppose nothing stays the same.' Despite her down-to-earth tone she felt a tinge of regret as she said those words, regret for those lost days when she had been so much in love with him.

She wondered who he'd gone to the restaurant with. Bianca maybe?

The notion crept up on her surreptitiously. After all, Luke had told her Bianca was in England now and that they were still friends. So it fitted that he might have dined with her. She tore her mind away from that thought. Luke could dine with a different woman every night; it was none of her business. 'Do you still have your apartment in London?'

Luke nodded. 'I rented it out while I was away in New York, but the tenant has recently left. I've just had it redecorated.'

'So you're going to keep the place?'

'I need it, Alison. Obviously my job will take me up to London and it's a good base.'

She wondered suddenly if Bianca was staying at the apartment? If their divorce was as amicable as Luke was making out that could be a possibility.

As Alison watched Luke across the table a whole scenario opened up in her mind. She imagined Bianca and Luke having a no-strings steamy affair. Could even see them at his apartment in the bed where she and Luke had once lain making passionate love.

Angrily she tried to concentrate on the conversation. Luke's personal life was nothing to do with her; why was she speculating so wildly and conjuring up these pictures? And more worryingly, why the hell did they hurt so much?

With difficulty she tuned her mind back to the conversation and tried to focus only on business-related aspects.

'As you'll be so busy with work and skipping backwards and forwards to London, I'm surprised you even have time to think about investing in the Cliff House.'

'Well, the Cliff House is more of a financial investment than a real time commitment.' He smiled at her. 'Don't worry, I wasn't thinking of coming in and offering to cook breakfasts.'

'I don't think Michael would be too happy if you were. He's in charge of the kitchen.'

'He's the one who is having the engagement party on Sunday?'

'Yes. He's marrying Susan Blake.'

'Oh, yes, I remember Susan. Her father was our estate manager for a while before he had to retire with ill health. She's a lovely girl.'

Alison nodded. 'Yes, she is. They make a good couple.'

'I'm looking forward to their party.' Luke reached and refilled her glass. 'I gather they are having it on Sunday because the hotel is busy with the wedding at the weekend.'

'That's right. But all the wedding guests will be gone by Sunday afternoon.'

'How are things at the hotel? Did Garth manage to deal with the arrival of the wedding party yesterday?'

'Yes, he did. He managed everything very well actually.'

'Which means you can take time off more often.' Luke grinned at her roguishly. 'Maybe I'll make it a condition of my investment; I'll have it written into a contract somewhere that, ''Alison Trevelyan is to be given lots of time off to spend with Nathan and me.'''

'I'm sure that would go down like a lead balloon with Garth.' Alison smiled. She knew he was only joking, and that his only concern was the amount of time he spent with Nathan. But she was touched that he pretended to include her in the premise. 'Anyway, you'll want to spend quality time alone with your son...so maybe it's best I'm kept busy.'

Luke was silent for a moment. 'But it would be nice if we could act more like a family...for Nathan's sake, don't you think?'

The gentle question opened up all kinds of emotions inside her, a searing sadness, and uncertainty and an absurd and tenuous feeling of hope.

They couldn't act like a family because they weren't one, she told herself sensibly. And yet as she looked across into Luke's eyes a picture was painted for one illusive moment of the three of them together.

'I think we'll have to be very careful not to confuse our son, Luke,' she said softly, trying very hard to maintain common sense. 'If we're too civilised…too friendly towards each other he's just going to wonder why we aren't together.'

'You mean we should prepare him for the day we marry other partners?'

The question made her heart turn over. 'I suppose so.'

She glanced away from the intensity of his eyes, not liking the question and definitely not wanting to think that far ahead.

In the silence that followed the waiter came to clear the table. 'Would you like another coffee?' Luke asked.

Alison shook her head. 'We had better go, Luke.' She was surprised by how much she regretted saying that. There was a part of her that would have liked to linger in the warmth of the candlelight, to turn the conversation back to the fantasy of her and Luke and Nathan being a real family. Or even just to the fantasy of Luke wanting to spend time with her…

Whatever had happened between them over dinner, it was almost as if time had turned back.

For just a little while the old ease that they used to have around each other seemed to have crept in, like a frequency on a radio band that kept tuning in for a little while before getting distorted again. Those clear and wonderful fragments were probably just an illusion brought about by the candlelight and the wine…yet she wanted to grab hold of them and keep them.

The drive home was quiet and Alison wondered what Luke was thinking about. She glanced across at him, taking advantage of the fact that it was dark and his concentration was firmly on the road.

What would it be like to have him back in her life?

she wondered suddenly. For them to go out like this as a matter of course, for him to be actively involved in bringing Nathan up?

What would it be like to reach over and touch him, kiss him?

Daydreaming like this was a mistake, she reminded herself as Luke pulled into her lane. She'd allowed herself to think she had something special with Luke once before and look how it had turned out.

Luke pulled the car to a halt outside the cottage and switched off the engine.

'Well, that was very pleasant.' She wondered if she sounded as breathless as she felt? Because the truth was that as she looked across at him in the darkness she very much wanted to move into the warm circle of his arms, just as she'd used to in the days when they had dated.

'Can I come in for a little while?' he asked.

She hesitated. The way she felt at the moment, inviting him in would probably be a mistake.

'I won't stay long,' he said quietly and she felt herself weaken.

'Well…OK, just for a little while.'

Jane was sitting by the fire in the lounge watching TV, but she switched it off immediately as Luke and Alison came in.

While Alison told her all about the restaurant and the food, Luke went upstairs to look in on Nathan.

'He's besotted by that little lad,' Jane said as Alison came to a halt.

'Well…yes.'

'I'm glad things are working out for you. He's a lovely man.' Before Alison could say anything in reply the woman had stood up and was reaching for her coat.

If she didn't say something now she would be married

off to Luke by the gossips in the village tomorrow, Alison thought. She followed Jane out into the hallway. 'Well, it's not really what it seems, Jane. My relationship with Luke is a bit complicated.'

'Oh, yes?' Jane paused by the front door.

There was silence as Alison tried to decide what to say. Then she met Jane's eyes and knew that all she could say was the truth. It would be out soon anyway and it was better coming from her. 'Luke is Nathan's father,' she admitted.

Jane smiled. 'I knew it!' she said delightedly, as if Alison had just told her she'd won first prize in a quiz. 'As soon as I saw Luke with that little boy I just knew it…couldn't understand why I hadn't figured it out before. He's the image of Luke! And of course I always knew that Todd wasn't his dad. I mean, the man is very nice but you can tell he's not really interested in Nathan. He's not very natural around him at all.'

There was a movement behind them and Alison turned and saw Luke standing in the doorway.

'I'm just telling Jane…our news.'

'Yes, so I heard.' Luke eyes were so serious as they held hers that she wondered what was going through his mind.

'Well, I'll get off,' Jane said brightly. 'And don't worry, your secret will be safe with me.'

'On the contrary, Jane,' Luke said, glancing over at the woman with a smile. 'You can tell who you want; it's not a secret any more.'

'I thought the situation needed clarifying,' Alison said lightly as the door closed behind Jane.

'Yes…it did.'

She looked over and met his eyes, feeling very awkward. 'So…everyone will know by tomorrow.'

'Good.' Luke's voice was decisive and pleased.

Was it good? Alison wondered as she went past him back into the lounge. No matter how hard she tried to grasp control of these circumstances she still felt extremely vulnerable.

'How was Nathan?' she asked as Luke went to stand with his back to the fire.

'Fast asleep.'

For a moment the only sound in the room was the soft crackle of the fire burning greedily around the logs.

'God alone knows what the gossip will be in the village about us tomorrow,' Alison sighed.

'Do you care what people say?'

'No. I just...I suppose I just want a return to some normality.' She sat down on the settee and swept a tired hand through her hair.

'It will soon die down,' Luke said with certainty. 'I'm more concerned about what Jane had to say concerning Todd.'

Alison frowned.

'She suggested that Todd wasn't particularly good around Nathan,' Luke pointed out drily.

'Don't start on Todd,' Alison warned. 'This is difficult enough...'

'So what is Todd's attitude towards Nathan?'

'He's fine,' Alison muttered dismissively. She supposed Jane was right; Todd wasn't that interested in Nathan. Oh, he was always kind and he tried...but there was no spark there. Not that it had ever mattered, because she had never really thought about the relationship deeply enough for it to matter.

'Just fine?' Luke drawled derisively. 'Don't you think if you are serious about Todd that his attitude towards Nathan needs to be a bit better than that?'

'Oh, for heaven's sake, Luke, just drop this subject. What are you going to do, grill every girl you date from here on in as to her attitude towards Nathan?'

'I'm hoping that's not going to be necessary.'

'Got the perfect woman in mind, have you?'

'I could have.'

The quiet confidence of his tone made her frown. Was Luke already seeing someone else? Or was this a reversal of what he'd told her about Bianca?

'You see, I don't think our situation needs to be as complicated as we're making it,' Luke said quietly.

'Doesn't it?' Alison got up from the settee and walked towards him. 'I don't see how you figure that.'

'Very easily.' Luke reached out to take hold of her hand. 'You see, I keep thinking about the past and how good we were together once.'

The touch of his hand and the softly spoken words were like liquid fuel igniting feelings inside her that she knew were dangerous.

'Thinking about the past isn't a good idea, Luke.'

'But I can't help it.' He moved a little closer.

'What we had was a fling—'

'Do you remember the first time we made love at my apartment?' Even as he was speaking she was aware that his head was lowering towards hers, and she was aware also that at any point she could have moved back. But she didn't; instead curiosity and desire held her hostage, and when his lips captured hers she felt heat and longing rise inside her with a fierceness that mocked all her words of protest.

For a few seconds she stood, helplessly vulnerable, while his lips moved over hers. Just don't kiss him back, she told herself. Prove to him and to yourself that all that old sexual chemistry has gone.

But as his hands moved up and over her body deliberately and provocatively, finding her breasts through the silky material of her dress and caressing them with a bold possessiveness, she felt heat rise like a tidal wave inside her and suddenly she was kissing him back with a passion and intense need that surprised even her.

She was breathless as he pulled back.

'You see…we still are good together,' Luke murmured. He cupped her face in his hands as he stared down into the bright, wide green of her eyes. 'When we kissed yesterday the old magic was instantly there…you felt it as well, didn't you?'

'No…it's wrong…it's just…'

'Just…sexual?' Luke smiled at her. His fingers caressed the softness of her face with a butterfly-softness that stirred answering flares of need inside her. 'Something that feels this good surely can't be wrong?'

As he kissed her again Alison was dazedly aware that she couldn't argue with that, or rather while she was enjoying the pleasure of his caresses she didn't want to argue with that.

He kissed the side of her face and his hands stroked up through her hair, before his lips hungrily fastened on hers again. She opened her mouth, allowing him access, surrendering to the wonderful feelings of arousal.

She felt the zip of her dress being pulled down, but she stood where she was even though there was a part of her that was urging caution. A part of her that knew this could only lead to more heartache.

But as he pulled her dress so that it slipped down slightly and his hands found the generous curves of her breasts in the soft, lacy bra the voices of caution were banished completely by much stronger instincts.

'You're so beautiful...Ali.' The huskiness of his voice made her insides melt. 'I want you so much.'

Her dress slipped a little more and she felt his hands against her skin. 'From the moment I set eyes on you again I've wanted to take you into my arms...and I've fought against it...really fought.'

His words caused tumultuous chaos inside her. She knew what he meant because she had felt like that as well.

'But what's the point of fighting this, Ali...when we could enjoy so much together...?'

His hands pushed her dress further down until it slipped to the floor and yet she felt no shame as she wound her arms up and around his neck, only a deep and overwhelming awakening of her senses. There had been no one for her since Luke...all her emotions and her needs had been firmly shut away and it was as if Luke was drawing back the bolts and unleashing feelings she'd forgotten she possessed.

His hands travelled over the curve of her bottom up towards the fastening of her bra. The feeling of his skin against her nakedness made her tremble with renewed need. She helped him to unfasten her bra and then shivered with acute delight as his fingers curved uninhibited over her breast. Then his head bent and he took one ripe and hardened nipple into the warmth of his mouth.

She groaned with an ecstasy that was delirious in its approval.

For a while they clung together as if they had been thrown together in storm-tossed waters, yet revelling in the ferocity of what was happening between them.

'You taste so good.' Luke's voice was uneven and the sexy depth of his tone turned her on even more. 'Shall we go upstairs?'

He didn't wait for her answer before his lips captured hers again. She felt his hands stroking her body, moving from her waist to the firm warmth of her breasts. The feeling was an ecstasy of torment, it was addictive and thrilling and she wanted more, so much more that it was shocking.

She wanted to go upstairs with him and lie between the softness of the sheets, feel his naked body against hers.

'Ali?' He nibbled at her ear. 'We've wasted so much time, let's not waste any more.'

CHAPTER EIGHT

THEY didn't bother to put the light on in her bedroom. Luke carried her over to the bed and put her down and then she watched in the half-light that streamed in from the landing as he started to get undressed.

He had the most perfect body, she thought, her eyes moving hungrily over the broad shoulders that tapered down to a flat stomach and lithe hips. Luke glanced over and caught her staring at him and smiled.

Damn man knew he was good-looking, she thought, turning away and taking off her shoes. This was probably a big…big mistake, she told herself nervously as she started to roll down her stockings. And it wasn't too late—she could still tell him she'd changed her mind.

He came over and knelt on the bed beside her and reached to help her remove her stockings. The provocative touch of his hand running down the inside of her thigh made all thoughts of calling a halt to what was happening disappear. She looked up into his eyes and her heart felt as if it were drumming in her mouth as his fingers moved to play with the lacy string of her pants. Then he drew them down and his fingers moved to stroke the soft, womanly core in a way that made Alison shudder with pleasurable sensitivity. She leaned back against the pillows and closed her eyes as wave after wave of pleasure flowed through her.

He was too good at this, she thought. The strong, sensible side of her didn't stand a chance. As he bent his head and his lips followed where his fingers had played she found herself gripping the bedclothes in an effort not to cry out with a need that tore to her very soul.

His lips moved up over the flat plains of her stomach, his hands holding and caressing her breasts before his mouth took over, licking them, biting them, and then as she groaned with delight he straddled her and took control of her lips, plundering her mouth, aggressively domineering her body now with an ease that only served to fuel her desire even more.

She made low moans of rapture.

'What are you saying to me, Ali?' he whispered.

'I'm saying I want you.' Her voice was heavy with desire. 'I really want you.'

His thumbs stroked over the sensitised peaks of her breasts, playing provocatively with her, and she felt the heat of his manhood pressing heavily against her.

'I can't hear you,' he whispered. 'You'll have to say it again...louder.'

'I want you.' Her voice lifted on a shudder as she felt him penetrate her. The full thrill of him made her senses reel with delight. Her hands raked over the strength of his back as he moved against her in a rhythm as natural and as old as time itself.

She could feel every nerve in her body responding to the dominance of his. The feelings of joy and bliss blocking out every other thought. She cried out his name as she reached the peak of ecstasy, and then he captured her lips, absorbing the last shudders and cries with a forceful possession.

Afterwards as they lay entwined in each other's arms Alison was too spent to talk or move. But she had never felt more content as she did in the afterglow of their love. The feeling of his arm warmly protective around her and the steady, rhythmic beating of his heart as she laid her head against his chest were soothing and soporific.

Vaguely she was aware of the soft patter of rain against the window. It felt and sounded somehow like the calm stillness after a storm. She put her arm around Luke and tried to cuddle even closer.

At some point she must have fallen asleep because when she opened her eyes she found herself covered by the bedclothes, with the warmth of Luke's body still pressed closely against hers. As the memories of what had happened between them returned she didn't know whether to be mortified by her wild abandonment or to give in to the rush of desire at feeling Luke beside her.

She remembered the way he'd told her he wanted her and that he'd tried to fight against it. Was there a chance that he really did have feelings for her?

As she lay there trying desperately to make some kind of sense out of the chaos of her thoughts she heard a sound from the room next door. She sat up slightly to listen. Nathan was crying.

Hastily she started to move to go to see to him.

'It's OK, I'll go.' Luke's deep voice next to her startled her.

'I didn't realise you were awake,' she said softly.

'I've been awake for a while.' He kissed the side of her face. 'Fighting with my conscience as to whether it was morally right to wake you from such a peaceful and deep sleep so we could make love all over again.'

She felt herself flush with heat and pleasure, the idea of an action reply arousing her immediately. Impulsively she reached up and kissed him softly and invitingly full on the lips.

Nathan started to cry again. 'I'll see to him.' She pulled away reluctantly.

'No, stay where you are,' Luke said gently. He kissed her on the forehead before pushing back the covers and reaching to put his trousers on.

As Luke left the room Alison rolled over onto her back and stared up at the ceiling. What was she doing? she asked herself. Hadn't she learnt her lesson with Luke?

She heard his gentle, reassuring tone as he spoke to their child and she squeezed her eyes closed in angry defeat. Even though she knew he didn't love her she was weak where he was concerned and she hated herself for it. But even whilst hating herself she couldn't seem to stop the feelings he aroused in her. Why was that?

The sound of Nathan crying again made her gather herself together and move swiftly out of the bed to investigate. She put on her dressing gown and moved silently towards the other room.

The crying had stopped again by the time she reached the open doorway. Luke had picked him up out of his cot and was rocking him gently, his tone soothing and reassuring.

The sight of him pacing backwards and forwards holding his son so tenderly stopped Alison in her tracks.

This was Luke's real objective…to be close to his son. Oh, there was no doubt that he had enjoyed sex with her last night. But it was a means to an end. What Luke wanted most of all was his son.

Why had she allowed him to seduce her so easily? she asked herself in anguish. She had known full well what it was all about…he hadn't even tried to lie to her, to pretend a love he didn't feel. He'd just relied on the fact that he could easily get any woman he wanted into bed and had used that power to get her exactly where he wanted her. That he had been able to do it so easily was humiliating in the extreme.

Nathan started to cry again, and motherly concern instantly took over. Pushing all other thoughts from her mind, she went further into the room. 'What's wrong with him?' she asked.

Luke glanced around and seemed relieved to see her. 'I don't know. He's very hot, Alison. I think he has a temperature.'

She took the baby from him, running a practised eye over him, noting his cheeks were red and he looked hot and uncomfortable. 'What's the matter with you, then, you little rascal?' she asked softly. He stopped crying as he was transferred into his mother's arms and tried to smile at her but it was a short-lived attempt at bravery before his eyes welled up with tears again and his face crumpled into more tears.

Alison put a gently soothing hand on his forehead and his cheeks. 'I think he's teething again,' she said. 'I've got some medicine downstairs, Luke; will you go and get it for me? It's in the fridge.'

'Yes, of course.'

As Luke disappeared down the stairs, Alison found Nathan's teething ring in one of the drawers and held it to the child's mouth. It seemed to placate the crying for a while, but Nathan was still unhappy.

'Do you think it is his teeth?' Luke asked in concern as he came back with the medicine.

'Yes, I'm nearly sure it is.' Alison smiled down at the toddler. 'We've had a lot of sleepless nights with these nasty, painful teeth, haven't we, darling?'

Luke watched the experienced and capable way she handled the child.

She glanced up and met his eye. 'It's all right, Luke. I'll manage now,' she said firmly.

'Am I to take that as a dismissal?' Luke's voice was wry.

She shrugged and looked away from him. 'You don't want to be around when Nathan is in this state.'

Luke reached up and touched her face. 'That's where you are wrong.' His words were low and disturbingly gentle. 'I very much want to be here, Alison.'

The touch of his hand and his voice made her feel lost in those few seconds and she couldn't even begin to know what to say. Then Nathan intervened, crying loudly and kicking his legs with impatience.

It took longer than Alison had thought to settle him. The crying grew louder and more intense and for almost an hour both she and Luke concentrated all their efforts to soothe him.

The first rays of sunlight were peeping through the nursery blinds by the time the child finally started to quieten.

'I think he's just overtired now,' Luke murmured, putting a hand on his son's face again. 'His temperature is down.'

She sat down on the arm of the nursery chair and glanced at Nathan, who was in Luke's arms by the side of his cot. It was obvious the little boy was no longer in pain but was simply battling against sleep; his eyes kept closing and opening again as he refused to give in.

'With a bit of luck we might be able to put him down soon,' she murmured tiredly.

Luke glanced up from his contemplation of the child and his eyes rested on her face, lit by the soft radiance of the nursery night-light. She was very pale, he noticed, and the shadows beneath her eyes gave her a gaunt, hollow appearance. 'You look tired, Ali,' he said gently. 'Why don't you go back to bed and get some rest? I'll stay with Nathan until he gets to sleep.'

And then what would he do? she wondered suddenly. Follow her back to bed, reach to hold her? Her heart turned over at the thought.

They had both been so busy over the last hour worrying about Nathan that there hadn't been any time for their own emotions, but now, as Nathan settled more contentedly in Luke's arms, the memory of what had happened between them returned to haunt her with forceful intensity.

What was she to do about this situation? she wondered with anguish. Obviously Luke didn't love her and she had been crazy to contemplate for even a moment that he might. She should never have slept with him; it was like letting a destructive and cruelly taunting genie out of the bottle again.

But there was no doubting his love for his son, his gentleness and his patience. Her eyes moved over the handsome features, the tender way he held his son so protectively in his arms, and she felt her stomach tighten painfully.

And suddenly the answer to why she had let him into her bed, the answer to why she had hoped so fervently that he might have feelings for her hit her forcibly. She was still in love with him.

'Ali?' He walked over and put a hand under her chin, tipping her face so that she was forced to look up at him. 'Are you OK?'

The gentle contact of his skin against hers was like an electric shock to her senses. She flinched away from him. 'Of course I'm OK.' Her tone was tightly controlled. 'You're right, I'm just tired.' She got up from the chair and moved away from him.

You are not in love with Luke Davenport, she told herself over and over again. You're not thinking straight, you're just exhausted and over-emotional.

'Why don't you take today off work?' Luke suggested. 'I'll ring Garth once it gets to a reasonable hour and tell him—'

'You'll do no such thing, Luke,' she cut across him. Honestly, the nerve of the man! He spent one night in her bed and he thought it gave him carte blanche to take over her life! Well, he had another thought coming. She didn't love him and she didn't want him interfering in her life. 'I'll be in my office at the usual time. Nathan is OK and Jane will cope.' She glared at him. 'And I don't need any help from you organising my life. I've managed for two years on my own with Nathan and I haven't done a bad job.'

'I never said you had,' Luke answered quietly. 'And I never doubted for a moment your ability to cope alone.'

Luke's calm tone took the heat out of her annoyance. He was only trying to help, she told herself, sweeping a hand through her hair. She was overwrought, and snapping at him like this wasn't helping.

'Yes, well…' She trailed off and met his eyes ruefully. 'Thanks for the offer but I'm all right.'

Luke shrugged. 'Just don't let Garth put too much on your shoulders today. That guy tends to take advantage of your good nature at the best of times.'

'That's rich coming from you,' Alison muttered.

Luke frowned. 'What's that supposed to mean?'

'Well, you were the one taking advantage of me last night.'

Luke laughed. 'Come on, Ali, that is stretching things a bit… I think if you cast your mind back you'll remember you didn't take that much persuasion; you wanted me last night every bit as much as I wanted you and we both enjoyed what happened.'

He watched her face flood with embarrassed colour. Then glanced down at his son. Nathan was almost asleep now. Quietly he went over to the cot and risked putting him down. The child moaned and stirred for a second but didn't wake up.

Luke smiled and gently tucked the blankets over the little boy. Then he turned his attention back to Alison, who was watching him intently.

'Shall we go back to bed and discuss this?' he asked huskily.

By the tone of his voice and the way his eye ran seductively over her body in the silk dressing gown, she had no doubt as to what he meant when he said 'discuss' things.

'Just keep away from me, Luke,' she warned, backing away from him nervously.

'I know you enjoyed last night, Ali…so why put up this pretence?'

He was so damn sure of himself, she thought angrily. 'Last night was just OK, Luke. I'm sorry if that dents your male ego, but it wasn't that good!' She smiled derisively.

Luke didn't appear the slightest bit taken aback by her words. He smiled. 'You can deride what happened between us as much as you want, Alison. But you and I both know that there's a powerful chemistry between us.' As she made to take another step back from him he caught hold of her arm. Then his hands moved to span her waist, drawing her closer.

The touch of his skin through the fine silk of her dressing gown was like a burning reminder of the power he possessed over her senses. Instantly she wanted to respond by moving closer, pressing her body close against his.

He bent his head and kissed her, a gentle yet compelling kiss that drew her emotions skilfully and poignantly to the surface.

She loved him and she couldn't deny it as a flood of searing sweet feeling teemed through her. For a second she allowed herself to respond and then she wrenched herself away from him, infuriated at herself for her weakness.

OK, she loved him, but she still had her pride. He may be able to turn her on and use his power over her emotions to his own advantage, but she wasn't going to let him have it all his own way. 'I think you had better go now.'

'If that's what you want.' He stepped back from her. 'I've got to go to London later but I'll be back before your brother's engagement party on Sunday. Can we talk then? Shall I pick you up at eight?'

She shook her head. 'I've already arranged to go with Todd.'

Luke's expression was wry.

'Don't look at me like that, Luke,' she muttered. 'Todd asked me to go to the party with him and I said yes... I'm not going to change my mind.'

'And what do you think Todd would say if he knew how we'd spent last night?'

She frowned. 'Todd isn't going to know because it's not worth mentioning.'

'Really? Well, I think it's worth mentioning.'

He watched the disconcerted expressions flickering

across her face and then smiled. 'See you Sunday, Ali…pleasant dreams.'

She watched as he checked on Nathan, brushing a gentle hand over the sleeping child's face before quietly leaving the room.

A few moments later she heard the sound of the front door closing and then the throaty purr of his car as he pulled away down the country lane.

Alison moved towards the cot and for a little while she watched tenderly over the sleeping child. Poor little thing didn't have a clue what was going on around him, she thought wretchedly, he had no idea that the two people who loved him most in the world were torn in pieces over him.

She stroked a stray curl from the child's forehead, remembering how concerned and how supportive Luke had been earlier when Nathan had been so fractious.

Then she remembered the heat of their lovemaking and squeezed her eyes closed to try and stop herself from thinking about it.

There was no way she could risk having Luke back in her life even for Nathan's sake, or the sake of just a steamy and passionate affair. The truth was she remembered too well how he'd hurt her once before. She couldn't trust him. He was going to London tomorrow and for all she knew tomorrow night would be spent with some other woman, maybe even Bianca…

The early-morning chorus of birdsong filled the silence of the room, rising with a joyous crescendo that seemed to mock the feeling of bleakness inside her.

CHAPTER NINE

'SO HOW was dinner with Luke?'

Alison's nerves stretched; she had been dreading Todd asking that question.

'Not too bad.'

'Is that all you are going to say?' Todd frowned.

She glanced across at him, regretfully. 'It was a bit tense,' she added but Todd was scowling at her.

'Oh, come on, Todd, give me a break,' she sighed. 'Garth has been interrogating me about Luke as well. And I'm really fed up with it. I'll tell you what I told him. Luke and I are making an effort to get along for Nathan's sake.'

'Have you seen him since you went out for dinner on Thursday night?'

'No. I haven't seen him or spoken to him since.' She decided not to mention the fact that Luke had been in London.

'But he's sent you flowers.' Todd's gaze moved to the magnificent bouquet that sat on the table behind them. The scent of the flowers seemed to overwhelm the room and they were a heady reminder of the man and what had happened between them.

Alison glanced from the flowers back to Todd. 'Yes, he sent me flowers.'

Unable to bear the conversation any longer, Alison got to her feet.

'I'll go and put the kettle on,' she said cheerfully. 'Make us some coffee.'

She stood at the kitchen sink, staring out at the back garden. It was Sunday morning, and she could hear the distant sound of the church bells from across the fields.

She had tried not to think too much about what had happened between her and Luke over these last few days. But she felt as if she was fighting a losing battle. He'd be back from London now and in all probability he would be at Michael's party tonight. The thought of seeing him filled her with a mixture of pleasure and apprehension.

The phone rang and she snatched it up.

'Hi, it's me.' The warm sound of Luke's voice sent her thoughts reeling into even further chaos.

'How are you?' he asked politely and she couldn't help but smile.

What would he say if she told him she couldn't even think straight because of him? 'I'm fine,' she said airily. 'Thank you for the flowers.'

'You're welcome. How's Nathan?'

'Playing happily in the lounge.'

'So no repercussions of our sleepless night?'

The gentle question sent sharp, bittersweet emotions racing. 'On the contrary, everything has been wonderfully peaceful.' Her answer was in direct opposition to the state of her emotions. Nathan had been sleeping soundly, but she certainly hadn't.

'I was just ringing to ask if you'd both like to come out today. I thought we could—'

'I'm sorry, Luke, but I can't. Todd is here.' She cut across him swiftly.

There was a moment of silence. 'Well, can't you get rid of him?' The question was asked gently, but it still irritated Alison.

'No, I can't!' she muttered, annoyed that he would

think she would drop everything at a moment's notice for him.

'OK…well, can I take Nathan out this afternoon?'

There was silence while Alison thought about this. In fairness she supposed that there was nothing to stop Luke taking out his son on his own. 'Well, I suppose so.' She gave in reluctantly.

'Great; I'll see you later, then.'

The phone went dead.

Alison turned as the kettle switched off. And wished suddenly that she had told Luke it wasn't convenient to see Nathan this afternoon. It wasn't that she thought she couldn't trust Luke with Nathan…on the contrary, she trusted Luke with her son more than she had ever believed possible. It was just that she didn't really want to be left behind. She felt as if she had effectively cut herself off from a place where she was meant to be.

'Who was that?' Todd asked as she brought the tray of drinks back through to the lounge.

'Luke. He wants to take Nathan out this afternoon.'

'Does he?' Todd brightened slightly. 'Maybe we could go out for lunch together, then?'

'All four of us?' Alison teased.

'Don't be silly.' Todd didn't even smile.

Nathan was at the other end of the room playing with his building bricks. 'Keep the noise down, will you, Nathan?' Todd said impatiently as the child knocked down a tower he had built with a boisterous yell.

Alison put her tray down on the table and passed Todd his drink. 'So what sort of a week have you had?' she asked before he could ask again about Luke or about going out for lunch. She didn't want to go out with Todd today; in fact, she wished he had rung before coming over so she could have put him off.

'Hectic. I need to take more staff on.'

Alison sat down and tried to listen with interest. But after a couple of minutes' hearing about the day-to-day running of his dental practice his words started to blur as her mind began to wander.

Todd was an attractive man, she supposed. He was probably about the same age as Luke and the same height with blond hair and hazel eyes.

So why did he fail to turn her on in the same way…why couldn't she feel excited in his presence, why didn't the sound of his voice make her feel warm inside? Her eyes drifted over the grey shirt he was wearing and the black jeans. He was smart and yet he needed something…maybe a good work-out in their gym to make his shoulders and his chest match Luke's. Luke had a very desirable physique.

As soon as the thought crossed her mind she was appalled. How shallow was that? She was a twenty-five-year-old woman and she was thinking like a schoolgirl. Looks weren't the most important thing in life. Todd had been a good friend to her.

Even so, the memory of Luke taking her to bed, making love to her, his powerful body pressed close against hers made her feel hot and feverish.

'Are you all right, Alison?' Todd asked, breaking off in mid-sentence.

'Fine.' She picked up the plate of biscuits and offered them across to him.

He shook his head and she put them back down.

'You look very pale if you don't mind me saying so.'

'Do I? I haven't been sleeping too well,' she admitted.

'Because of Luke?'

'No, of course not,' she lied.

Todd put his coffee down. 'So what about coming out with me this afternoon, then?'

Nathan wandered over and knocked into the table at that moment, causing coffee to jolt over the polished surface.

'Now, that's very silly!' Todd said sternly, wagging his finger at Nathan, who looked at him in startled amazement. 'You need to be more careful, young man.'

Suddenly the differences between the way Todd acted around Nathan and the way Luke behaved seemed to jump out at her in stark contrast. Todd was so stilted and he really had little patience.

But that didn't matter, she told herself fiercely, because she was happy just being friends with Todd and she didn't need him to be a father to Nathan.

The words rang hollowly inside her, though. Was she happy spending time with Todd? He was a nice man and had been very supportive in the past, but why had she never wanted to take their relationship further, as she was sure Todd wanted to? Why had she always made excuses to fend off Todd's subtle advances?

Because she was still in love with Luke, the words resounded inside her painfully.

Alison got up to get some paper towel so that she could mop up the coffee. She needed to stop thinking like this, she told herself sharply. Luke didn't love her so it was best to forget about him, and comparing him with Todd was unfair. Todd was her friend.

'You know, this situation with Luke might be to our advantage.'

Alison looked across at Todd blankly. 'How do you mean?'

'Well, think about it; Luke will probably want Nathan to live with him for part of the time. We'll be able to go out more and enjoy ourselves, clubbing and party-ing—'

'Todd!' She glanced over at him with a light of an-guish in her eyes. 'I don't want to lose Nathan for part of the week. Don't you understand, the thought horrifies me?'

'You'll get used to it.'

'No, I won't,' Alison said firmly. 'And, anyway, I don't think Luke would cope. He's not used to having a baby around.' But even as she was saying those words she doubted their truth. Luke seemed very capable around Nathan.

'If I know anything about Luke he'll have an attrac-tive blonde on hand before too long to help him out,' Todd said with a grin.

If that was supposed to be funny, Alison wasn't laugh-ing. But she supposed Todd was right.

'So about lunch?'

'I can't, Todd. I've got a whole pile of paperwork waiting for me. And I'd like to get it out of the way so I can enjoy Michael's party tonight.' It wasn't a lie— she did have paperwork to do. She was still working on her idea for the gym and she wanted to get all the figures and the questions involved clear before presenting them to her brothers.

Todd shrugged. 'Well, OK, I'll go down to the pub and enjoy a pint. What time do you want me to pick you up tonight?'

The sound of a car pulling up outside the house dis-tracted Alison's attention. 'That can't be Luke, surely?' she muttered, glancing at her watch. 'He said he'd come this afternoon. It's only just gone eleven o'clock!'

The shrill ring of the doorbell cut through the house.

'Shall I go and investigate?' Todd asked.

'No…I'll go.' She hesitated. 'Just keep an eye on Nathan for a moment.'

As she went out into the hallway, closing the lounge door behind her, the doorbell rang again.

'OK, I'm coming,' she muttered, running a smoothing hand down over her hair.

Somehow she wasn't surprised that it was indeed Luke standing on her doorstep.

'You're early,' she murmured, trying not to notice how handsome he looked in blue jeans and an open-necked white shirt.

'Am I? It's such a pleasant, sunny day I thought we might as well get out before it clouds over. You don't mind, do you?'

As he walked past her into the hallway the scent of his aftershave brought immediate memories of their night together crowding in on her in a deliciously sensually shivery kind of way.

'No…I don't mind. But I haven't got Nathan ready for you.' She felt acutely self-conscious as she looked up and met his eyes.

'That's OK, I can wait.' In contrast to her he seemed perfectly at ease. His eyes swept over her with an intense scrutiny that brought even further awareness flooding through her. It was as if he could see through the sheer blue blouse she wore to the lacy underwear beneath.

'Well, as I told you on the phone, Todd is here. So…so I'd appreciate it if you were nice.'

'Nice?' One dark eyebrow rose sardonically. 'To Todd?'

'Yes.'

Luke shrugged. 'You're asking me to do something that really goes against my natural instincts, Alison.

Have you told him about us yet?' The sensual, husky tone brought her immediate palpitations.

'There is no ''us'',' she hissed, slanting a nervous look towards the lounge doorway. 'Keep your voice down.'

'I take it that means you haven't told him?'

'I don't want to discuss this, Luke,' she said firmly. 'Just be cordial to Todd and refrain from stirring things.'

'I'm always cordial.' Luke looked amused. 'But as for stirring things, well, I'm sorry but the idea of Todd just seems to bring out the worst in me.'

'Luke!' Her eyes narrowed on him. 'This isn't a game.'

'OK, I'll be nice, but there is a price attached,' Luke murmured, a teasing light in his eye.

Alison looked at him suspiciously.

'At least two dances at the party tonight,' he said firmly.

Despite the tension inside her Alison smiled. 'You're crazy, Luke Davenport.'

'So have we got a deal?'

She looked up into his eyes. 'OK, two dances,' she murmured huskily.

'With a third open to further negotiation.' His voice was deep and sexy and she felt as if an invisible web of desire was drawing her in.

Suddenly the door was wrenched open from the lounge, breaking the curious intimacy.

'Everything all right?' Todd looked from one to the other of them.

'Todd, old chap, nice to see you,' Luke said jovially as if he were greeting an old friend. 'How are you?'

Todd looked slightly taken aback by the exuberance

of the greeting. As well he might under the circumstances, Alison thought wryly.

'I'm fine, thank you.' His reply was stilted.

'And how's the dental practice going—not too many
extractions, I hope?'

'Good dental work eliminates the need for extractions,' Todd muttered seriously.

'Great, so everyone's happy.' Luke slanted a wry look
at Alison and ignored her narrowed warning look.

Nathan came running out into the hallway at that moment, a smile on his face as he saw Luke, but before he
could reach his dad Todd swept him up in his arms.

'So where are you taking our little tiger today?' he
asked.

Alison's eyes widened at the comment. 'Our little
tiger'? Why was Todd talking like that? Never in all the
time she had known him had he referred to Nathan so
possessively.

If Luke noticed the possessive vernacular he didn't
show it. 'There's a travelling funfair at the other side of
town—I thought we might nip over and have a look and
an ice cream.'

'Sounds fun.' Todd ruffled the child's hair. Nathan
was having none of it; he was obviously not comfortable
in Todd's arms and squirmed wildly to get down. Giving
up, Todd let him escape and he toddled happily over
towards Luke, who swung him high above his head,
making the child giggle helplessly with pleasure.

'I'll just get his coat and his pushchair for you.' With
reluctance Alison left the two men alone as she went
upstairs for Nathan's clothing.

When she returned the men were no longer in the
house. She glanced out of the open front door and saw

them standing in the lane talking, Luke holding Nathan in his arms.

She hoped Luke wasn't saying anything untoward. She didn't want to hurt Todd; he was a good friend and Alison was sensitive to the feelings he had for her. If he had to know about what had happened between her and Luke, she wanted to be the one to tell him. Hurriedly she went out into the sunshine to join them.

However, she needn't have worried; the men were talking about Luke's car, a brand-new expensive silver saloon car that was parked on the grass verge.

'Where's your sports car?' Alison asked in surprise as Luke opened the boot and took the pushchair and bag from her to store them safely.

'I've traded it in.' Luke met her eyes. 'Decided my life needed certain changes to make it more child-friendly.'

'I see.' Alison tried not to look as taken aback by this piece of news as she felt. Luke was certainly serious about all this...

'We'll probably be back around five,' Luke said as he brought Nathan around and strapped him into his car seat.

'OK.' Alison leaned forward to give Nathan a kiss. 'Be good for...Daddy.'

As she pulled back and Luke closed the door she met his eyes. There was a strange kind of unspoken communication between them in that moment.

'See you later.' He smiled at her and then turned away to get into the car.

Todd slipped his arm around Alison's waist while they watched him pull away, but she was barely aware of the gesture; she was too busy wishing she were in that car with her family.

'Right, well, I'll get off to the pub and leave you to your paperwork,' Todd said. 'And I'll see you tonight.'

'Yes.' She looked over at him. 'What was all that tiger business about, by the way?'

Todd smiled wryly. 'I just couldn't resist.'

'Couldn't resist what?'

'I wanted him to know he's not the only one who cares for Nathan.'

'Oh, Todd!' She looked up at him, quite touched by the words.

'I know I'm not particularly good around kids, Alison, but I do care for him...and for you.'

'Todd.' Alison stopped walking and turned to look at him. 'I think you should know—'

'That you are still in love with him,' Todd cut across her abruptly. 'I know.'

'What do you know?' Alison stared at him, really taken aback by his words, wondering if Luke had said something after all.

'I know you've never stopped missing him, wanting him.' Todd shrugged. 'I kind of hoped at first that we would make a go of it, but I resigned myself long ago to just having your friendship. I still don't like seeing him walk back into your life so easily, though; it kind of grates on me.'

'It's only because of Nathan...' Alison faltered, trying to make things easier on both of them.

'Yeah.' Todd didn't sound as if he believed that for one minute. 'But I noticed the way you were looking at each other a moment ago. Be careful, Alison. I saw how he hurt you once before; don't let it happen again.'

'Of course it won't happen again—'

'I feel I should tell you Alison. Luke Davenport was

seen in the pub last night with one of the girls who work on your hotel reception desk. Clare Fisher.'

The words sent a shadow of disquiet rolling through her. 'Was he?' She shrugged and tried to look as if she didn't give a damn. 'Well, he's a free agent; he can see whoever he likes.'

'I suppose so.' Todd looked a bit uncomfortable. 'I just thought you should know. It's only because I care about you, Alison.'

Alison was sitting at the kitchen table, paperwork spread in front of her. But despite her best efforts it was hard to concentrate.

Had Luke been out on a date last night with Clare?

She remembered how the other woman had smiled at him at the hotel. And her words to describe him—'He's drop-dead gorgeous.'

Women were always flinging themselves at Luke. It didn't necessarily mean he was dating her.

She frowned; why was she trying to reassure herself? It didn't matter what was going on in Luke's life. It had nothing to do with her.

Todd's words kept repeating in her mind. 'I saw how he hurt you once before; don't let him do it again.'

Impatiently she got up and poured herself a glass of water. She wasn't going to let Luke hurt her...she was older and wiser; she'd learnt her lesson. Yet the memory of their lovemaking was vivid and intensely unsettling.

What did he want from her, she wondered; a cosy little affair on the side that would let him come and go around Nathan as he pleased? She'd already told him she wouldn't stand in his way of seeing his son. Maybe he was just intent on getting rid of Todd. Clearing the decks so he could have more control of the situation. That could be why he had shown some interest in the hotel as well. By investing in it he'd have even more influence over her and therefore over Nathan.

That idea made her angry. Well, Todd was wrong when he said she was letting him back into her life too easily. She wasn't going to make anything too easy for Luke.

She put her glass down and went back to concentrate on the papers on her table. Suddenly it seemed imperative to make her idea for opening their gymnasium to the public work. She needed to ensure Luke didn't get too powerful a stronghold around her.

Alison was making good headway with the work by the time she heard Luke's car outside. And somehow it made her feel better about everything, as if she was taking back some control over her life.

Nathan had fallen asleep in the car and he didn't wake up as Luke lifted him out.

'Have you had a good afternoon?' Alison asked cheerfully as she opened the door to him.

'Yes, we have.' His eyes swept over her as he stepped into the hall. 'You should have come; we missed you.'

She tried to ignore that and also disregard the fire he was instantly able to start inside her. 'I was busy.'

'Todd's gone, I take it?'

'Yes.' Alison looked at Nathan; his cheeks were rosy and his lips curved in a smile. 'How long has Nathan been asleep?'

'About half an hour; I'll go and put him down in his cot.' Luke turned towards the staircase. 'If you are making a coffee I'd love one,' he said over his shoulder with a grin.

She went into the kitchen and put the kettle on. Then started to tidy away her papers.

'What have you been doing?' Luke asked as he came in.

'Just a few accounts for the hotel.' She bundled them back into her briefcase.

'Is it a secret?' he asked, an amused glint in his blue eyes.

'No, I just don't like to leave things lying around.'

'Is it to do with your idea for the gym?'

She turned to look at him then, her eyes narrowed. 'How do you know about that?'

'Oh, I've got my sources around here, Ali,' he said with a smile. 'You know, you'll have to get permission from the council if you want to open up to the public.'

The casual remark made her feel very ill at ease. 'I realise that and I have everything in hand.'

'Good for you.' He smiled. 'If you need any help I could have a glance over your paperwork?'

'I don't need any help, thank you.' She watched as he leaned back against her kitchen counter looking the epitome of cool confidence and it really disconcerted her. She hadn't wanted him to know about her plans until she was ready to tell him. 'So who told you about my ideas for the gym?'

'Garth. I bumped into him and his wife, Sonia, this afternoon. We all had lunch together; it was very pleasant.'

That news sent further disquiet through her. 'You two seem to be getting very friendly all of a sudden.'

'Surprisingly we get on very well. Maybe we both realise how foolish we were in the past.'

She turned to make him a coffee. 'So what else did you talk about apart from my project?' she asked curiously.

'Did we talk about you, you mean?'

'No, I don't mean that.' She looked around and caught the gleam in his eye.

'Well, I'm not going to tell you what we talked about because you should have been with us.'

'I was busy, working.'

'Well, at least you weren't wasting the afternoon with Mr Personality,' Luke said drily.

'Don't, Luke,' she warned, handing him his coffee. 'I hate it when you start pulling Todd to pieces.'

Luke met her eyes. 'But you've got to admit the guy has no sense of humour,' he remarked matter-of-factly.

'Yes, he does. You've just got to get to know him.'

'I'd rather not.' Luke took a sip of his coffee and then put it down on the counter beside him. 'In fact, I want to forget Todd Johnson ever existed.' He reached out and, taking her by surprise, pulled her into his arms, holding her firmly trapped against him. 'But you've got to admit I was very courteous to him today.'

'Too courteous.' Her heart stared to drum chaotically at his close proximity.

He gave her a slow smile. 'I can't win with you, can I?'

'Why do you want to win?' she asked cautiously.

'Because I don't like losing…because I enjoyed what happened between us the other night.' He pulled her a little closer. 'Because I want you…right now.'

'I think you are playing games with me, Luke,' she murmured, trying not to give in to the weakness that immediately stole through her body.

'I'm not playing games; in fact, I don't think I've ever been more serious.'

'When did you get back from London?' She tried to keep herself apart from him.

Luke frowned. 'Yesterday afternoon. Why?'

'I just wondered.' She shrugged. 'Someone saw you in the pub last night with Clare.' She couldn't help her-self—she just had to ask him.

'Clare who?' he murmured, his gaze intent on her lips.

'Clare who works on Reception in the hotel.'

'Oh, her; yes, I think she was there—the place was packed.'

He leaned his head down and took possession of her lips in a teasing and thrilling kiss that made her lean against him with wanton disregard for the fact she had been telling herself that she wasn't going to do this, wasn't going to give in to this desire again.

'I really didn't like leaving you the other night, you know,' he whispered against her ear. 'I wanted to take you back to bed, hold you close, whisper sweet nothings in your ear.'

'You are a consummate smooth talker, Luke...' Her voice was huskily unsteady as she tried to be sensible, but he cut the words off in mid-flow, kissing her again with a passion and intensity that made her forget what she was thinking besides what she was saying.

She felt his hands moving over her body, touching her through the gossamer-fine blouse. And instantly she was aroused. She felt him pulling her top from the waistband of her jeans and then his hands were on her naked skin, smoothly encompassing her narrow waist.

'You want me, too, don't you?' he whispered.

She shut her eyes and tried to tell herself that she didn't but the word 'liar' was screaming through her subconscious.

Then his mouth covered hers again, expertly plundering, turning her on so much that she felt incoherent with need.

She wound her hands up and around his neck, returning the kisses.

The front fastener of her bra was unhooked and he took her breasts in both his hands, his fingers teasing over them. Her breathing was coming in short, sharp gasps of pleasure.

The sound of Nathan crying suddenly filtered downstairs and they both stilled. She looked up into Luke's eyes, so blue that they seemed to drown her. 'Saved by my son,' she whispered, trying to make a joke of her state of undress, and of the fact the Luke's hands were still possessively and warmly over her half-naked body.

His thumbs stroked over the hardness of her nipples. 'We'll have to carry this on later, then.'

She closed her eyes on a stab of desire and longing.

'Come to the party with me tonight?'

'I can't. I told you I've already promised to go with Todd.' She struggled to concentrate on being strong.

'Then make some excuse to him and come home with me afterwards.'

'I can't, Luke!' She wrenched herself away from him. 'That wouldn't be fair on Todd.'

'Sleeping with me the other night wasn't exactly fair on Todd either,' Luke murmured softly.

He watched her face flush with colour.

'That was a mistake.'

'No, it wasn't,' he said softly. 'You should finish with Todd and come home with me tonight.'

'You've got it all figured out, haven't you?' she asked shakily.

'I know we need to have some time alone to work things out between us.'

'If I went home with you the only thing we'd be working out was how long it takes to get undressed.'

'What's wrong with that?' he teased.

'Everything.' She wrenched herself further away from him and started to tuck her blouse back into her jeans. 'My life is well-ordered and I'm happy, Luke. I don't want the kind of emotional chaos you bring. I don't trust your motives…I don't trust you.'

'Why, because of that business with your property three years ago? Come on, Alison—'

'It's not just because of that…it's everything.' She looked up at him, her eyes filled with anguish. How could she tell him that she felt he was only interested in her because of Nathan? And that every time he so much as smiled at another woman she felt it cut deep inside. She didn't even know if she totally believed him when he said he couldn't remember who Clare was. So how could she start to rebuild a relationship with him again when she felt like that?

'What's everything?' he grated harshly.

Nathan's crying became louder. 'Nathan wants out of his cot. You should go now.'

'Yes, OK, I'm leaving. But I'm serious about us needing to talk.'

She hurried away from him towards the staircase. 'Just go, Luke,' she called back. 'There's nothing more to say.'

Nathan was standing up in his cot waiting for her and the moment she stepped into his bedroom the tears stopped and he smiled and raised his arms to be lifted out of his cot.

'You are just like your daddy,' she said with a shaky smile as she picked him up and gave him a hug. 'But just be warned,' she whispered. 'Using emotional weaponry to get your own way doesn't always work.'

And it wasn't going to work for Luke, she told herself fiercely. Just because he held some sway over her feelings didn't mean he was going to win control over her.

CHAPTER TEN

THE ballroom at the Cliff House Hotel was already packed to capacity when Todd and Alison arrived. There were streamers hanging from the ceiling and pink helium balloons with 'Congratulations to Michael and Susan' written on them. A band played on the stage at the far end of the room and the dance floor was thronged with people dancing.

'This is all very lively for a Sunday evening,' Todd said, glancing at his watch. 'You don't think it's going to go on too late, do you, Alison? I've got to be up early tomorrow to be at the practice at eight.'

'No, I don't think it will be too late.' Alison took a couple of glasses of wine from the tray of a passing waiter and gave one to Todd.

He smiled at her. 'Thanks.'

They moved a little further into the crowd. Alison's dress was blue Thai silk and the material shimmered as the lights of the ballroom caught it. Expertly cut, it clung lovingly to her figure, emphasising her curves in a very flattering way. A few men glanced over at her admiringly as she walked past but she was oblivious to them.

Surreptitiously she was searching the crowd for Luke. She kept telling herself that she hoped he wasn't here and yet she wasn't sure she was being entirely truthful with herself because when she couldn't see him anywhere there was a feeling of disappointment.

Susan and Michael were standing by the bar area chat-

155

ting with Garth and Sonia, and they made their way across towards them.

'Isn't it a wonderful turn-out?' Susan said excitedly as she hugged Alison. 'I think everyone is here.'

Susan had short blonde hair and was petite and bubbly. Alison really liked her, thought she was exactly what her tall, dark, serious brother Michael needed.

'Well, you are a very popular couple,' Alison said. 'Let's have a look at your ring again.'

Susan waggled her fingers, and a solitaire glistened under the lights.

'It's beautiful.' Alison smiled at her future sister-in-law. She had never seen Susan look quite so radiantly lovely.

As she looked up she noticed Luke had arrived and was talking with Garth. He was wearing a dark suit with an open-necked dark blue shirt, and he looked so handsome that she felt all her strong, sensible ideas of keeping well away from him start to waver.

'Your turn next, Alison,' Susan said quietly.

'My turn?' Alison looked back at Susan, momentarily losing what she was saying.

'To get engaged.'

'Oh, I don't think so!' Alison laughed that suggestion away. 'No, the next celebration in this family will be Sonia and Garth's baby.'

Luke was congratulating Michael; she could hear the two men chatting amiably. He was so close now that she could smell the subtle tang of his aftershave with all its evocative memories. Then he turned to speak to Susan.

She smiled happily up at him and reached to kiss him. 'It's really nice to see you, Luke,' she said warmly. 'Thanks for coming.'

'My pleasure.' Luke glanced over at Alison and

smiled. She made a lukewarm attempt to return the smile, the memory of how steamy their kisses had been earlier and the way his hands had moved so possessively over her body mocking her.

'Do you want to dance, Alison?' Todd asked her suddenly. She nodded, glad of the excuse to get away.

The music the band was playing was a slow ballad and Todd put his arms around her, drawing her closer.

'Can you believe the nerve of that guy, coming here?' he muttered against her ear.

Alison didn't need to enquire to whom he was referring.

'Luke was invited to the party,' she reminded him gently.

'He still has a nerve.'

'How did you enjoy your pint at the pub today?' Alison swiftly changed the subject.

'It was OK; I met up with Ellen, one of my receptionists.'

'Oh, yes. The glam blonde who has her eye firmly on you.' Alison smiled. 'Is she here tonight?'

'I think so.' Todd looked a bit embarrassed by the subject. 'But she's a colleague, Alison, she hasn't got her eye on me and even if she had I don't want to get involved with anyone at work—it just causes complications.'

'If you say so.' Over his shoulder Alison saw the woman in question at the bar; she was looking over in their direction.

'And don't try to change the subject; we were discussing Luke Davenport.'

'Were we?' Todd's receptionist was now making her way across to speak to Susan and Michael.

Todd swung her around. 'Yes, we were. So am I right, are you still in love with him?'

'My feelings for Luke are a bit complicated,' she muttered. She glanced up at Todd but now it was his turn to be distracted. He was looking over her shoulder with a faraway expression in his eyes.

'Bloody hell, I don't believe it!'

'What?' It was so unlike Todd to swear that she thought something was terribly wrong. 'What is it?'

'He's talking to her now!'

'Who?'

'Luke bloody Davenport is talking to Ellen.'

'Oh!' Alison had to laugh.

'What's so funny?' Todd glared down at her.

'I thought you said you weren't interested in Ellen?' She fixed him with a playfully amused look.

'I'm not. I just don't trust Luke Davenport.'

'Yes, well, they are only talking, Todd.'

They moved around to the music and Alison glanced over herself. They were talking quite animatedly, she noticed. Luke was laughing at something she was saying and looking at her very intently.

But whether it was Ellen or Clare...or Bianca...she didn't care, Alison told herself firmly. Luke Davenport could do what the hell he wanted. She was drawing every protective barrier she possessed around herself.

'Shall we go back to the bar and have another drink?' Todd asked after a while.

'OK.' Alison allowed him to take hold of her hand and lead her back.

Ellen had disappeared now and Luke was talking to Sonia. She was telling him that her baby was due in another week. 'So if I have to leave suddenly you'll know what's happened,' she joked.

Alison smiled at her sister-in-law as she reached to pick up her glass of wine.

'I just hope Garth is a bit calmer than when Alison was having Nathan. Do you remember, Alison? He nearly crashed the car when he was taking you to the hospital.'

'Will I ever forget?' Alison smiled and sipped her wine. Over the rim of the glass she saw Luke's eyes resting on her contemplatively.

'Don't listen to them, Luke,' Garth said as he came across to join them. 'I got Alison safely there.'

'I just hope you are going to be calmer when it's my turn,' Sonia muttered.

Alison took another sip of her wine and realised she had finished it.

'Another drink?' Todd asked quietly against her ear.

Alison smiled gratefully at him. 'I'll come to the bar with you,' she said, wanting to get away from the conversation.

As she stood behind Todd amidst the jostle and crowd of the bar she glanced back at Luke; he was talking to Clare now.

She was willing to put money on the fact that he had no difficulty remembering her name now, Alison thought drily. Clare was very attractive. Very slim and tall with a boyish kind of figure that made her look like a model. She suited the very short cut of her hair, and the black dress had a sexy dip at the front.

She was probably much more Luke's type, Alison thought. He went for blondes. Bianca was blonde.

As if he felt her watching them, Luke glanced over at her, an inscrutable expression in his eyes. She glanced away quickly in case he thought she gave a damn...

because she didn't, she told herself sternly. She really didn't.

'Here we are.' Todd handed her a glass of white wine.

'Thanks.' She took a couple of quick swallows.

'He's talking to Clare Fisher now,' Todd remarked. 'The man gets around, doesn't he?'

'Well, it's a party, Todd.' She took another sip of her drink, berating herself for sounding so coolly indifferent when she had been thinking exactly the same thing a few minutes ago.

'Don't look now but he's coming over here,' Todd muttered, making Alison almost choke on her wine.

'Thought we'd have that dance now, Ali.' Luke stopped beside them with a smile. 'You don't mind, do you, Todd?'

Without waiting for a reply Luke reached out and took Alison's glass of wine from her and, leaving her no time but to send an apologetic glance back at Todd, he led her away towards the dance floor.

'I don't particularly want to dance, Luke,' she said defiantly as he turned to face her once they were out on the floor. But it wasn't strictly true; what she didn't want was for her resolve to weaken if he took her into his arms.

'I thought we had a deal, Alison—at least three dances, remember?' He smiled provocatively. 'You're not reneging on it, are you?'

Someone jostled her from behind and she found herself in his arms as they moved to the melody of a love ballad.

'I think you'll find that the deal was two dances,' she murmured.

He smiled. 'You look lovely tonight, by the way.'

'Thank you.' She tried to hold herself stiffly apart

from him but it was difficult on the crowded floor. 'But I wonder how many women you've said that to tonight.'

'Only one.' He smiled. 'The band is good, don't you think?' he murmured, bringing her in a little closer.

'Yes. It's Susan's cousin's band.'

The scent of his aftershave was very pleasant, not overpowering, but just alluringly subtle.

'These family contacts are quite handy, aren't they? Speaking of which, Sonia was telling me that Nathan is staying around at her house overnight.'

'Yes, with Sonia's mother Phyllis. It was good of her to offer to babysit, otherwise I don't think I'd have been able to come tonight. Jane was invited to the party so I didn't like to ask her.'

'Yes, I saw Jane over by the bandstand with her husband.'

'We thought it was better if Nathan slept over so that Phyllis isn't waiting up for me.'

'So you have your freedom tonight.' Luke smiled.

The quiet remark made her remember his earlier enticements to get her to leave with him.

But to her relief he didn't pursue the subject. Maybe he realised he wouldn't persuade her to go home with him no matter what he said. Or maybe he'd already made contingency plans to leave with Clare? The thought sent a violent stab of jealousy searing through her. She was being ridiculous, Alison told herself angrily. Her imagination was taking over...for all she knew, all he'd done was talk to Clare...nothing more.

Alison leaned her head against the softness of his dark jacket. She remembered the last time she had danced with Luke at a party in London. That evening she'd had no hesitation going home with him. She had often thought about that night…wondered if it was when Nathan was conceived.

She felt Luke's arms tighten protectively around her as they moved. It was a wonderful feeling being in his arms; she had always enjoyed dancing with him, being held so close, so possessively. There was something extremely sensual about it. She closed her eyes; just for now she'd throw all the suspicious thoughts away and enjoy the pleasure of the moment.

It was just a dance after all, she told herself. What harm could a dance do? It wasn't as if he was going to start making love to her here in the middle of the crowded floor.

The music changed and blended into another slow tune and they continued to dance.

Luke moved his head down so that his lips were close to her ear. 'I hope you realise that this only counts as one dance, not two,' he murmured teasingly.

She smiled. 'I think that's cheating,' she replied, but she was in no mood to pull away. It occurred to her that if she moved her head fractionally they would be able to kiss.

'I meant what I said today about wanting you.' Luke whispered the words softly. He moved her long hair back from her face with a gentle caress, his hands touching her face.

The contact sent shivers of desire through her.

'Why are you fighting against this so much?'

'I told you this afternoon.'

'You don't trust my intentions?'

'I'm not the same girl you went out with in London, Luke.' She looked up at him, her eyes shadowed. 'I'm older and wiser and I have no time for a furtive little affair.'

The music changed abruptly and it was a relief to be forced to move away from him as everyone around them started to dance to a faster beat.

'Thanks for the dance, Luke.' Politely she moved away from him. Her heart was thudding painfully as she retraced her steps back towards the bar.

Garth handed her glass of wine to her as she reached him. 'Todd's on the dance floor,' he said.

'Thanks.' She glanced back towards the floor but couldn't see Todd amongst the crowd, although she saw Luke being waylaid by Clare.

'So how are things going with you and Luke?' Garth asked cheerfully. 'You looked very cosy on that dance floor.'

'Well, looks can be deceptive.' Alison turned away from watching Clare fluttering her eyelashes up at Luke and gave her full attention to her brother. 'He wants to rekindle our affair.'

'But you don't?'

Alison was silent for a moment. 'It would just end the same way, Garth. He doesn't love me, he wants Nathan…and he wants Todd out of the way. That's his motivation.'

'I wouldn't be too sure about that. He seems pretty genuine to me.'

Alison took a sip of her wine. 'He seemed pretty genuine when I went out with him in London. But as soon as I left he was dating someone else.'

'That doesn't mean to say his feelings for you haven't changed. Maybe he realises his mistake.'

Alison nodded. 'And maybe he never really loved me.'

She glanced back to where Luke was still talking to Clare.

'If you still love him it might be worth taking a chance on the relationship again, Alison,' Garth said quietly. 'Especially as you have Nathan to think about.'

'Who said I still loved him?' she asked gruffly.

Garth smiled. 'Well, don't you?'

'No, I don't.' Slanting a look up at Garth, she noticed he wasn't fooled at all. 'And I wish you hadn't told him about my plans for the gym.' Swiftly she changed the subject, feeling foolish and unhappy.

'I don't think there's any harm done. He thought it was a good idea and he told me he definitely wants to invest in the hotel—'

'Garth, you told me you'd hang fire with that for a while. We might not need him at all.'

'No, we might not. But I still think it would be good to have him on board. He's a very talented business-man.'

'He's obviously got you under his spell.'

'I like him, Alison, and I'm not afraid to say I was wrong in the past. Michael and Ian both agree with me as well. We all think he should come into the business.'

'So I'm just being overruled?'

'No, we think your plans for the gym are great. Luke thinks they are as well. He feels that—'

'I don't want to hear you quoting Luke right at this moment, Garth.' Alison put her glass down. 'If you'll excuse me I think I need some fresh air.'

As she pressed her way through the crowds of people suddenly all she could think about was getting out of here. Everything felt as if it was closing in on her…and it felt as if Luke had invaded every quarter of her life, every inch of her soul.

There was a side-door open and she slipped through it out onto the terrace.

It was a beautiful evening; the moon was big and full in a star-strewn sky. And although the breeze that cut in from the sea was cool it had lost that biting, wintry feel. She walked further along the terrace, away from the sounds of revelry, and then on impulse she stepped out onto the lawn and walked further away from the hotel towards the sea, seeking further solitude.

Stopping by a copse of oak trees, she leaned against one of the trunks. The sound of the ocean breaking against the rocks below was soothing. She had done the right thing turning down an affair with Luke, she told herself firmly. She had to remember what had happened in the past and only a fool went back for more.

'Lovely out here, isn't it?' Luke's deep, husky voice made her whirl around in surprise.

'Are you following me?' she asked unsteadily. 'Because if so I'd like you to leave me alone. I've come out here for some peace and quiet.'

'So have I,' Luke said calmly. He looked past her towards the sea. 'There's a wonderful view from here, isn't there?'

'Yes.' She turned away from him. He was right—it was a beautiful view. The sea sparkled jewel-bright in the light of the moon and the spray that hurled up against the rocks was highlighted a ghostly white against the black of the jagged cliffs.

'The beach down there used to be used by smugglers in the old days,' Luke told her conversationally as he walked past her. 'Apparently they landed their boats here and then used a network of caves that go right around towards the village.'

'Relatives of yours, were they?' Alison asked drily.

He flicked her an amused look. 'Not to my knowledge.'

She shrugged. 'Well, you certainly seem to be adept at moving stealthily into the core of my family. You've only been back in the village a week and they all seem to have fallen under your mesmerising charm.'

'Except for you,' he said quietly, turning to look at her.

'I know you better than they do.'

He smiled at that. 'Well, I should hope so.'

'And I've learnt from my mistakes,' she said positively.

He moved closer towards her. 'And I've learnt from mine,' he said quietly. 'I should never have left you with Todd Johnson.'

'You're just jealous of his involvement in your son's life.'

'Maybe.' Luke shrugged. 'But I don't think he's right for you either.'

He came closer. 'I know you said you don't trust me, Ali, but my intentions are honourable.' He reached out a hand and touched her face. She moved nervously away from the caress.

'And when you think about things logically we are both of the same mind...neither of us relishes the thought of standing on the sidelines watching someone else bringing up our child. You don't even want Nathan to have a different name from yours.'

She smiled wanly; she might have guessed he was still worrying about that. 'I've got a solution to that dilemma,' she said sardonically. 'You can change your name to Trevelyan...problem solved—'

'Here's an even better solution.' Luke cut across her flippant words with a calm seriousness. 'You can change your name to Davenport.'

'Change my name?' She frowned. 'By deed poll, you mean?'

'I mean we could get married.'

The words were so coolly spoken that for a moment she wondered if she had misheard them.

In the startled silence all she could hear was the rapid beat of her heart and the wild pounding of the surf against the rocks below.

Desperately she tried to read his expression, but his face was in shadow and she couldn't tell what he was thinking.

'Think about it; it's the perfect solution,' Luke continued evenly. 'We both love Nathan, we both want the best for him—'

'Marriage isn't quite as simple as that, Luke.' Her voice when she found it sounded remarkably detached and yet that wasn't how she was feeling. In truth there was a furnace alight inside with confusion and anger and maybe a touch of sadness, because if he had said this to her two and a half years ago she would have fallen into his arms.

'It could work if we wanted it to.'

'And what about the fact that we don't love each other?' Her voice was a mere whisper in the silence.

There was a heartbeat of a pause. Then Luke's gaze moved to her lips. 'But we know we are sexually compatible.'

The words were like a small explosion on her senses.

'I know you badly want Nathan in your life, but this is ridiculous. Marriage is enough of a challenge for people who really love each other…we wouldn't stand a chance—'

'I disagree. In fact, the more I think about it the more I think it would work. I could give you a lot, Ali…you certainly wouldn't have to worry about money again. You and Nathan could have a secure home…what could be better than for our son to have both his parents under the same roof…surely that's an ideal situation?'

'Not if we don't love each other it's not.' Alison felt angry suddenly, angry that he could suggest something as loving as marriage in such a cold and businesslike way.

Luke moved closer. 'Let me prove to you that things could work between us,' he said softly. 'All I'm asking is that you give things a chance.'

She shook her head. But before she could say anything he was closer. She leaned back against the bark of a tree behind her as he bent his head and kissed her.

The kiss was long and slow and so passionate that she felt all her senses reeling in disarray.

But how could she agree to his proposal…? she wondered hazily. How could she even contemplate marrying a man who didn't love her?

'Will you think about this?'

'I'm not ready for marriage to anyone, Luke. Let alone you,' she said breathlessly. 'And in case it's escaped your notice I'm seeing Todd.'

Luke held her eyes steadily with his. 'I think if you were serious about Todd you'd have married him by now. And what's more I think you haven't married him because you know he's not right for Nathan.'

His eyes raked over the pallor of her skin, luminescent in the moonlight. 'We'd make a great team, Ali,' he added gently. She could feel his breath on her lips; feel the now familiar twist of desire stir inside her.

'Don't, Luke!'

'Don't what…tell you I want you?' His eyes moved over her, taking in the way her chest lifted and fell under the stress of her breathing. His eyes moved to her eyes, holding them steadily with his. 'I can't do that, Ali. I've tried to stay away…but I can't stay away any longer.'

She shook her head. This was her opportunity to tell him she had given him his answer and that it was a categorical no. But she couldn't say the words, because there were voices inside her urging her to say yes.

'Come back home with me and we'll talk about it.'

He bent his head and kissed her again, a sweet and tormenting kiss that made her melt.

The sudden sharp crackle and bang of fireworks made them both pull apart in surprise. Glancing back towards the hotel, Alison saw the bright glitter of a Catherine wheel light up the night sky.

'The fireworks are starting,' she murmured, noticing a lot of guests coming out onto the terrace to watch the display that her brother Ian had set up for Susan and Michael.

'I thought they had already started,' Luke said huskily as she looked back at him. 'So what do you say; shall we give our relationship another chance?'

'I think you must be very serious about Nathan if you'll even contemplate getting married for him,' she said.

'Of course I'm serious about him!'

The whizz and fierce bang of a rocket zooming overhead drowned out their words and as Luke shifted away from her slightly to look up she took the opportunity to pull away from him.

'Well, it's not enough…Luke,' she said fiercely. 'It's not enough to make me want to marry you.'

The acrid smell of gun smoke hung in the air and a pall of mist swirled over the trees. It stung Alison's eyes and caught at her throat as she hurried away from Luke back towards the hotel.

CHAPTER ELEVEN

ALISON searched the crowd for Todd as she reached the terrace. But she couldn't see him anywhere.

Garth was by one of the doors into the ballroom and like everyone else his attention was fixed firmly on the sky and the glittering display.

'Garth, have you seen Todd anywhere?'

'No. He was standing by the bar last time I saw him,' Garth said, hardly shifting his eyes from the fireworks. 'Isn't this a fabulous display?'

'Yes, wonderful.' Alison moved past him back into the ballroom. She was in no mood to watch fireworks.

There were hardly any people left in the room and the lights had been dimmed so as not to reflect outside.

Alison made her way carefully around some tables. She was about to pick up her bag from beside the bar when a movement from one of the alcoves made her glance around.

Todd was there with Ellen. They had their arms wrapped around each other and were kissing.

For a second Alison was so startled she just stood rooted to the spot. Then silently she went to retrieve her bag and hurried out towards Reception.

There was no one on the desk so she went around and picked up one of the phones to call herself a taxi.

She was in the process of dialling the number when Luke appeared in the doorway.

'What are you doing?' he asked, coming further across towards her.

'Phoning a taxi.' She looked away from him, trying to concentrate on what she was doing and block out everything else.

Calmly Luke leaned across the desk and took the receiver from her hands. 'I'll give you a lift,' he said coolly. 'I'm leaving now anyway.'

'There's no need.' Stubbornly she was about to lift the receiver again.

'Don't be stupid, Ali,' he muttered.

She probably would have continued to argue with him but Clare came through from the ballroom.

She smiled at Alison. 'Shouldn't Paul be on Reception tonight?'

'Yes, but he's probably outside watching the fireworks,' Alison murmured. 'I was just ringing for a taxi.'

'And I was just offering a lift,' Luke said.

'Oh! You wouldn't be going anywhere near the village, would you, Luke? I'd love a lift, too,' Clare gushed. 'I've got to get home and get some sleep—I'm on duty early tomorrow.'

'Sure.' Luke reached to help her as she put on her coat.

'Thanks.' She smiled up at him, looking flushed.

'Come on, then, ladies,' Luke said equably as he headed out the door.

Alison hesitated for a moment and then, as Luke stood holding the side-door open for them both, she picked up her bag and followed.

'Aren't you waiting for Todd?' Clare asked Alison in surprise as they walked across the car park towards Luke's vehicle. 'I thought you would be going home with him.'

'Not tonight.' Alison's reply was cursory; she wasn't

about to reveal why she wasn't waiting for Todd. But as Luke slanted a dry look over at her she had the feeling he already knew the answer to that particular question. He'd probably seen Todd as he walked through the ball-room.

'I am surprised,' Clare continued blithely, seemingly unaware of the tense atmosphere.

Luke unlocked the car with a press of a button and deliberately Alison sat in the back, leaving Clare to the front passenger seat.

'It's been a wonderful evening, hasn't it?' Clare sighed as the car moved smoothly down the drive. 'I just wish I could have stayed later.'

'That's the downside of working shifts, I suppose,' Luke said.

As Clare continued to chatter inconsequentially Alison realised that the woman was slightly tipsy, and every now and then her words slurred and she giggled.

Alison smiled and leaned her head back against the comfortable seat of the car. She'd probably had a few glasses of wine too many herself. Maybe Todd had been a bit drunk as well? Must have been to relax to the point where he was kissing Ellen like that. It was about time Todd made a move on Ellen, she thought wryly. It was ridiculous the way he kept denying his true feelings be-cause they worked together.

The only person who seemed completely sober this evening was Luke. She stared out at the country lanes and tried not to think about Luke or his proposal. She'd done the right thing turning him down, she told herself staunchly. Living in a marriage without love would be torture. Every time Luke even glanced at another woman she would wonder if this would be the one to take him away. Even for Nathan's sake she couldn't live like that.

They reached the outskirts of the village and the car slowed. 'You'll have to direct me from here,' he said to Clare.

'Second turning on the left,' she murmured, sounding suddenly sleepy.

Luke followed the directions and then stopped outside a terraced cottage. As Clare struggled to get herself together Luke got out of the car and went around to help her.

'Isn't he just gorgeous?' Clare whispered to Alison in a giggly undertone.

Fortunately Alison was spared having to answer that because Luke had opened the door and was helping her out.

'See you tomorrow, Alison.' Clare waved at her.

'Yes, see you tomorrow, Clare.' Alison watched as Luke walked with her up to the front door and helped her to open it.

Clare laughed and leaned against him. Then as Alison watched she reached up and kissed him.

Hastily Alison averted her eyes, a rush of jealous adrenalin seeming to swamp her. Her hands tightened in her lap and she looked pointedly the other way. She was going to have to let go of Luke, she told herself forcefully. She couldn't keep feeling like this.

'Clare was slightly smashed, I think,' Luke said as he got back into the car a few minutes later, a note of amusement in his deep voice. 'It seemed to just hit her as she got out of the car and the air struck her.'

'She's probably tired; she was on duty very early this morning.' Alison forced herself to reply, but her voice was strained and edgy.

'Are you going to come and sit up front with me?' Luke asked, glancing at her in the rear-view mirror.

'No, I'm fine in the back.'

There were a few moments of hesitation and then Luke slipped the car into gear and drove away.

Silence hung heavily between them as they headed back out of the village, and without Clare's inconsequential chatter the tension between them was palpable.

Alison stared at the back of his head. She wondered what he was thinking. She wondered if she hadn't been here whether he would have gone inside with Clare and stayed.

The idea made her squeeze her eyes closed in anger.

'Are you angry with Todd?' The quietly-asked question made her eyes fly open again.

'No. Why would I be?'

'Come on, Ali. I saw him, as I'm sure you did.'

She shrugged. 'Todd can do as he likes,' she said airily.

Luke slowed the car.

'Why are we stopping?' Alison asked, looking around. They were about three miles from her cottage.

'I can't talk to you while you are in the back of the car. Why don't you get up front with me?'

'I'd rather not. Just take me home, Luke.'

But Luke brought the car to a complete standstill. Then to her consternation he got out and opened her passenger door.

'Luke, what the hell are you doing?'

'If you don't get in the front with me, I'll get in the back with you.' Luke bit the words out tersely. 'Because quite frankly, Alison, I'm so busy trying to look at you in the rear-view mirror that I'm going to crash the car.'

Hastily Alison stepped out of the vehicle. 'I'll just walk from here, then, thank you,' she said stubbornly.

Luke caught hold of her arm as she made to turn away.

'Look, I can understand that you are angry with Todd. But I don't know why you are taking it out on me. I've asked you to marry me, Alison, and—'

'Oh, and you think that makes everything all right, do you?' She glared at him.

'Well, I thought it might at least prove to you that I'm not just after a casual affair.'

'You had your chance to prove that to me almost three years ago, Luke Davenport, and you failed.' She glared at him and all of a sudden her eyes filled with tears. Embarrassed, she turned away from him. 'Anyway, I'm going home; just leave me alone.'

To her disquiet he fell into step beside her as she walked away. As she glanced sideways at him he held up his hands. 'Well, I can't let you walk home on these dark country roads on your own, can I? If anything happened I'd never forgive myself. So you either get back in the car or I'm walking with you.'

She stopped then and turned to face him. 'You've been out of my life for a long time, Luke. I don't know why you are trying to make out that you're suddenly concerned about me.'

'Because I regret being out of your life, Ali...regret it bitterly. And for what it's worth I never thought of what we had as just a casual affair and if I led you to believe that I'm sorry.'

The soft words played havoc with her fragile emotions.

'That night when we broke up, I was angry seeing you with Todd.' Luke's voice was low now and very serious. 'And I was hurt by what you said to me. But I shouldn't have walked away just because of my pride.

If I'd hung around instead of rushing off to New York I would have discovered for myself that you were pregnant…and that's going to haunt me for the rest of my life.'

A gust of sea air swirled around her, whipping her hair across her face and making her shiver suddenly.

'But even in America I never stopped thinking about you, Alison…never.'

'You didn't bother to come and see me when you came home almost twelve months later,' she said quietly. 'In fact, if Garth hadn't told you about Nathan I doubt you would have bothered this time either.'

'But I wanted to see you.' Luke moved closer. 'Of course I wanted to see you.'

She stared up at him with disbelief. 'So why didn't you?' she whispered. 'When I heard you were in the village I wondered if you would come.' Her voice wavered slighted, before she admitted huskily, 'I hoped you would come. But you returned to the States…you married Bianca.'

'And it was a mistake.' He whispered the words softly. 'And one of the reasons it didn't work out was that I couldn't get you out of my mind. When I came home last time I came to find you. Then I saw you with Todd. You were pushing a pram, you looked like a happy couple and I assumed…' He trailed off and raked a hand through his hair. 'I wrongly assumed the baby was Todd's. And the gossip in the village seemed to confirm that. I felt I had no right to barge back into your life, when you were obviously so happy. But I wanted to, Ali.' His voice was husky with feeling. 'I really wanted to.'

'Are you just saying this?' Her voice was very unsteady now and she felt her defenses starting to crack.

'No, I'm not just saying it.' His voice was gruff. 'I thought you were happy, Ali, and I told myself that I had to get on with my life. So I returned to the States and really tried to make a go of things.'

A tremor raced through her body.

'Come back to the car, Ali, you're shivering with cold and we can't talk out here.'

She allowed him to put his arm around her and together they headed back towards the vehicle.

As she settled herself in the front passenger seat Alison's mind was clouded and confused.

She wanted so much to believe what he had just said. But she was so scared of being hurt again, scared of falling for a line he chose to spin just because he wanted his son.

Luke turned the engine on and adjusted the heating so that some warm air filtered into the car. Then he glanced over at her.

'Will you come home with me?' he asked quietly. Then he held his hands up from the wheel of the car and gave a wry grin. 'Promise I'll behave like a perfect gentleman.'

Suddenly she was transported back to that evening when he had taken her to his apartment for the first time. 'Isn't my reply to that supposed to be, I don't want you to behave like a gentleman?' She smiled hesitantly over at him, wondering if he would remember that night.

He smiled back. 'So how do you want me to behave?' he murmured and, leaning across, he kissed her lightly on the lips. 'Am I heading anywhere in the right direction?' he murmured, pulling back and holding her eyes with his.

The words were so evocative that she felt her eyes

shimmer with tears. 'You've got a very good memory, Luke Davenport,' she whispered softly.

'For important things.'

He slipped the car into gear and they set off down the country road again.

If this was a mistake then suddenly she didn't care, Alison thought as she sat watching him. She was tired of fighting with her emotions. She wanted to believe that he had missed her...wanted to forget the pain and just remember the good times, and there had been many of those.

He turned the car up into the Davenport drive, and after a while the house came into view, its lights glittering in the darkness.

'Home, sweet home.' Luke smiled at her and got out of the car.

It seemed even colder outside now and the wind was getting up, whipping her dress and her hair wildly about her. As she hesitated by the front steps Luke reached for her hand and together they went inside.

The house was warm and silent. They made their way across the vast hallway towards the living room. A few side-lamps lit the darkness and the fire still burned in the grate.

Luke threw on some more logs as she sat down on the settee.

Allison had never been more conscious of Luke; how handsome he was, how self-assured...and how much she wanted him.

'Would you like a drink?' Luke asked quietly.

She had probably had enough to drink but she nodded. 'A glass of wine would be nice.'

He had offered her a drink that first time at his apartment, she remembered. But she had barely taken one sip before they were in each other's arms.

He walked across to the sideboard and poured her a glass of red wine from the decanter. Then he placed it before her on the coffee-table, before moving to stand back by the fire.

She was surprised that he didn't sit next to her.

'Alison, I realise that you are probably only here with me because you're upset about Todd,' he said softly. 'But my proposal of marriage was genuine and it still stands.'

She frowned. 'I'm not upset about Todd.'

'You don't have to put a brave face on it for me, Ali. I understand.'

'Do you?' She stared up at him.

'Yes…you probably would have married Todd long ago if it hadn't been for Nathan and the fact that the two of them don't seem to get along too well—'

'They get along OK.' She got up from the settee and walked closer towards him. 'But I don't really want to talk about Todd,' she said with gentle impatience.

As she reached his side she stood on tiptoe and kissed him softly full on the lips. He reached out and caught hold of her around the waist, and then he drew her against him, kissing her back with a fierce passion that made her breathless with need.

For a few wonderful moments they stood wrapped in each other's arms, the only sound the crackle of the fire.

'Ali, stop.' He was the one to call a halt to the proceedings, pulling away from her with an abruptness that stunned her.

'I meant it when I said we needed to talk.'

He paced away from her to the other side of the fireplace. 'Firstly I want to talk about what happened between us in London. I'll admit when I first started to go out with you all I was looking for was an affair. But you became much more important to me than that.'

She sighed and pressed a shaking hand against her lips, which felt swollen and heated from his kisses. 'You don't have to lie to me, Luke. I want to make love with you anyway.'

There was a silence between them that seemed to stretch forever.

'But that's just it, Ali. I'm not lying to you. You see, I'm probably the biggest fool to ever walk this earth, but when we were dating in London I didn't quite realise what I'd found with you...oh, I knew I was besotted, that I couldn't get enough of you.'

He watched her closely. 'But until you went back to Cornwall I didn't realise just how much I loved you.'

The softly spoken words made her angry suddenly. 'Don't, Luke! Don't lie to me about that. Not now... please!'

Ignoring her, he came closer towards her again. 'What is it they say...you never realise just what you've got until you lose it?' He murmured the words huskily and, reaching out, he traced a line down the side of her face with infinite, delicate care.

It made her tremble inside with acute need and she longed so much to believe him. 'So if you missed me so much after I left London, why did you go out with Bianca?'

He frowned. 'I didn't go out with Bianca until a long time after we finished.'

'What do you call a long time? Two weeks after I left your bed?'

'No!' He grasped her arms, holding her still as she made to swing away from him. 'Alison, look at me.'

When she refused he took hold of her chin, forcing her to meet his eyes.

'I started to date Bianca after I moved to the States. There was nothing but friendship between us before that.'

'That's not what she told me on the phone.'

Luke frowned. 'Well, when the hell did you speak to her on the phone?'

'After I learnt that your father had bought our house; I rang you the very next day at your apartment…at seven in the morning and she answered…said she was your girlfriend, said you were in the shower.'

Luke was looking at her as if she were talking another language. 'Well, that's just rubbish! Yes, I offered Bianca my apartment…but only when I wasn't there. I was in the States on business.'

'So why did she say you were in the shower? That you were her boyfriend?' Alison was blazing now as she remembered her shock and her heartbreak after that phone call.

'I don't know, Ali.' He drew away from her and she could tell from the look on his face that he was shaken by her accusations. 'I don't know why she said that. But she was lying. I never laid a finger on Bianca Summers until a couple of months after I was living in New York. We got on well together because of work…I missed you and I was determined to get over you and she was…there.'

He watched the way her eyes narrowed. 'I know that's not a very admirable thing to admit, Ali…but she threw herself at me and she was warm and beautiful and I was lonely.'

'But it happened in London,' Alison maintained staunchly.

'No, damn it, it did not.' Luke glared at her and the fury in his eyes made her feel suddenly as if she had made the biggest error of judgement in her whole life.

'She either lied to you…and quite frankly it wouldn't be the first time that Bianca had lied in her life.' Luke raked a hand through his hair. 'Or you misheard her.'

Alison shook her head. 'I was angry that morning but I definitely didn't mishear what she said. And it was in our local paper that you might be getting engaged to her. There was a picture of you attending some charity function with her.'

'Crikey, Alison. You can't believe everything they write in that damn rag!' He glared at her. 'I'd have been married a hundred times over if all that stuff were true.'

'Well, I believed it.' Her heart slammed against her chest painfully. 'We were miles apart…you had her in your apartment—'

'Er, excuse me, but I think you had better rephrase that remark or I'm going to get even more seriously annoyed.'

'Yes, well, the evidence was stacked against you, Luke.' She stared up at him. 'And you did marry her.'

He nodded. 'Because she told me she was pregnant.'

The quiet words stilled Alison.

'I thought we could make a go of it… I was genuinely fond of her. You were settled…or so it seemed, with Todd.' He raked a hand through his hair. 'After the wedding I found out that she wasn't pregnant at all, she admitted lying to me, we had an argument in which she accused me of still being in love with you and I stormed out.' For a second Luke's eyes were darkened with memory. 'I did try and put things back together with her after that. We were married and I do believe in the sanctity of marriage and I did care for her…so I thought it was worth trying to work things out. Then one day I came home early and found her…let's say in a compromising position with a work colleague.'

'Luke, I'm so sorry!' Alison was horrified.

He shrugged. 'At the end of the day we just weren't right for each other. And at least we were able to realise that fact before we tore each other apart. In the end our separation and our divorce were remarkably civilised and we have been able to stay friends…we both made mistakes, and we both recognise that.'

'I really thought you loved her…' Alison whispered tremulously. 'You even admitted that what we'd had was just a fling that last time I saw you—'

'Because my pride was too great to do anything else…' he interrupted her fiercely.

'There were rumours flying around that you were going to announce your engagement—'

'Yes, but I wanted to announce my engagement to you…I'd come to ask you if you'd go away to New York with me.' He cut across her abruptly. 'But when I returned to Cornwall I discovered you'd already committed yourself to the hotel…and you were seeing someone else. You told me I meant nothing to you…and I was so angry I just agreed with you that our affair meant nothing.'

'You really wanted me to go away with you?' She felt suddenly as if she had stepped into a dream. That any moment now she was going to wake up and be cruelly disillusioned.

He nodded. 'I loved you, Alison…I've never stopped loving you.'

'I thought you only wanted me now because of Nathan.' She whispered the words unevenly.

'I adore Nathan, and I want to be a good dad to him,'

Luke said steadily. 'But I reckon I could still do that without marrying you. I want to marry you because I love you, Alison.' He stroked a strand of her hair back from her face. 'I know you don't feel the same...that Todd is the man you really want, but—'

'I don't want Todd.' She cut across him powerfully. 'Oh, he's a nice enough guy, but he's just a friend. And I'm not upset that he was with Ellen earlier. I'm happy for him.'

He moved even closer. 'But I thought your love for him was what made you turn down my proposal?'

She shook her head. 'I love you, Luke...I've always loved you.' Her voice broke slightly. 'I just never thought you'd return my feelings and—'

Whatever else she had been going to say was cut off as he reached to kiss her.

It was a long time before they pulled apart.

'You really don't have feelings for Todd?' Luke asked her again as if he could hardly believe her.

'He's always been just a good friend,' she said firmly. 'We've never even slept together,' she admitted huskily. She watched the relief and the pain in his eyes.

'I'm so sorry I doubted you, Luke,' she whispered, looking up at him. 'I've been so unhappy without you. And so jealous...every time you even glance at another woman I feel myself heating up inside like a volcano. Tonight when Clare reached to kiss you I felt...' She trailed off. 'I can't find the words to explain how I felt; it was awful.'

'I think I might kind of know that feeling,' Luke murmured softly. 'I've felt it every time you've mentioned Todd's name.'

He tucked her closely against him. 'You're all the

woman I'll ever want.' He whispered the words softly. 'So will you marry me?'

She felt her eyes welling over with tears of happiness. 'Yes, Luke, I will.'

Their kiss was gently passionate and so all-consuming that Alison felt quite dizzy as they drew apart.

Then Luke swept her off her feet and before she realised his intention he was carrying her out of the room and up the stairs to his bedroom.

She laughed breathlessly as he put her down in the deep comfort of his double bed. And she thought he was going to join her immediately. She was surprised therefore when he pulled away and went over to a beautifully inlaid bureau at one side of the room.

'What are you doing?' she asked as she sat up impatiently to watch him opening the drawer.

'Getting you your wedding present.'

'Wedding present?' She frowned. 'Shouldn't that wait until we get married?'

'I think it's waited long enough.' He took out a large envelope and turned to put it down on the bed beside her.

'What is it?' Curiously she opened it and took out the documents inside.

'It's the deeds to your farm…the place where you grew up.'

She looked up at him wordlessly.

'I bought the farm…not my father. My full name is John Luke William Davenport. I bought the farm because I knew how much you loved it and I thought you'd regret losing it…and I thought it would be an incentive to make you come to New York with me. That you wouldn't feel so bad being in the city if you knew you were coming back to the place you love most of all.'

Alison bit down on her lip and tears sprang suddenly to her eyes. 'You really did that for me?'

He nodded. 'Only when I found you with Todd I had too much damn pride to tell you.'

'I'm so sorry, Luke.' She whispered the words tremulously.

He joined her in the bed and flung the papers down on the floor. 'At least we got one thing right in the past,' he murmured before he possessed her lips. 'We got Nathan.'

She nodded and cuddled closer, adoring the feel of his body, hard and loving, against hers. 'Tell me again that you love me,' she whispered. 'I've waited so long to hear you say those words that I still can't believe them.'

'I love you, Alison Trevelyan, even though you are the most stubborn, pig-headed, irritating woman I've ever met in my life.' He punctuated all the words with kisses and she smiled up at him.

'A true Davenport in the making, you might say?'

'Yes…speaking of which…' He started to unfasten her dress and reached over to switch out the light.

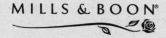

MILLS & BOON®

Modern Romance™

THE MILLIONAIRE'S REVENGE by *Cathy Williams*

Years ago Laura had been passionately involved with Gabriel Greppi. But he'd shocked her with a proposal of marriage and she'd turned him down. Gabriel has never forgiven her, and now he's a millionaire while Laura is on the verge of bankruptcy. He plans to seduce her and then reject her – as she rejected him. But will it be so easy…?

STAND-IN MISTRESS by *Lee Wilkinson*

Brad Lancing may be a successful businessman, but he has a bad reputation when it comes to women. Joanne Winslow is determined that her sister will not become just another notch on Brad's bedpost – even if it means she'll have to become his mistress herself!

THE MEDITERRANEAN TYCOON by *Margaret Mayo*

Peta is struggling to juggle single motherhood with the demands of her new boss, Andreas Papadakis. And then the Greek tycoon makes a surprising offer. He needs a live-in childminder, and for the sake of her own son Peta is tempted to accept. She takes a chance on living with the boss – only to realise there's more on his mind than a professional relationship…

THE MATCHMAKER'S MISTAKE by *Jane Sullivan*

When future psychologist Liz Prescott meets Mark McAlister she decides he's presenting her with the perfect opportunity to practise her matchmaking skills. Once his transformation is complete he can have any woman he wants! But as Liz sees the alpha male emerge from beneath Mark's reserved exterior she has to admit she wants him for herself…

On sale 1st November 2002

Available at most branches of WH Smith, Tesco, Martins, Borders, Eason, Sainsbury's and all good paperback bookshops.

1002/01b

Don't miss *Book Three* of this BRAND-NEW 12 book collection 'Bachelor Auction'.

Who says
money
can't buy
love?

On sale 1st November

2 FREE

books and a surprise gift!

We would like to take this opportunity to thank you for reading this Mills & Boon® book by offering you the chance to take TWO more specially selected titles from the Modern Romance™ series absolutely FREE! We're also making this offer to introduce you to the benefits of the Reader Service™—

- ★ FREE home delivery
- ★ FREE gifts and competitions
- ★ FREE monthly Newsletter
- ★ Exclusive Reader Service discount
- ★ Books available before they're in the shops

Accepting these FREE books and gift places you under no obligation to buy, you may cancel at any time, even after receiving your free shipment. Simply complete your details below and return the entire page to the address below. *You don't even need a stamp!*

YES! Please send me 2 free Modern Romance books and a surprise gift. I understand that unless you hear from me, I will receive 4 superb new titles every month for just £2.55 each, postage and packing free. I am under no obligation to purchase any books and may cancel my subscription at any time. The free books and gift will be mine to keep in any case.

P2ZEA

Ms/Mrs/Miss/Mr ....Initials.................................
BLOCK CAPITALS PLEASE

Surname ....

Address ....

....

....Postcode......................................

Send this whole page to:
UK: FREEPOST CN81, Croydon, CR9 3WZ
EIRE: PO Box 4546, Kilcock, County Kildare (stamp required)